THE MAGIC WORLD

EDITH NESBIT (1858–1924) was a mischievous, tomboyish child who grew into an unconventional adult. With her husband, Hubert Bland, she was one of the founder members of the socialist Fabian Society; their household became a centre of the socialist and literary circles of the times. The chaos of their Bohemian home, managed by the restless 'Daisy' (as she was known to her friends), was regularly increased by the presence of numerous friends, among whom were George Bernard Shaw and H. G. Wells. And apart from their own children, Edith also raised two adopted children.

Her clothing, haircut, lifestyle and habit of expressing herself forcefully and in public proclaimed her to be a woman who was trying to break out of the mould which English society demanded at the time. She was no armchair socialist, however: in fact, despite her success as a writer, late in life her charitable deeds brought her close to bankruptcy.

E. Nesbit – she always used the plain initial for her writing, with the result that she was occasionally thought to be a man – turned late to children's writing, after a number of years as a successful writer of short pieces for adult magazines. Thanks to her success, she was approached by a popular children's magazine of the time to write pieces about her childhood.

This request opened up a rich vein. When Edith turned from describing the literal facts of her childhood to capturing in fictional form the happy and relaxed atmosphere she had known as a girl, the result was a series of children's books which have remained firm favourites and bestsellers for decades. One of her most admired abilities as a writer is the combination – often with more than a pinch of humour – of a real-life situation with elements of magical fantasy. *The Magic World* displays this Narnia-like combination at its best in a dozen stories – a dozen enchanting spells with magical animals, sorcerers and princesses, Justnowland and other fantastic places.

Some other Puffin Classics to enjoy

THE ENCHANTED CASTLE
FIVE CHILDREN AND IT
THE LAST OF THE DRAGONS AND SOME OTHERS
THE STORY OF THE TREASURE SEEKERS
NEW TREASURE SEEKERS
THE PHOENIX AND THE CARPET
THE RAILWAY CHILDREN
THE STORY OF THE AMULET
THE WOULDBEGOODS
E Nesbit

E. NESBIT

The Magic World

PUFFIN BOOKS

PUFFIN BOOKS

Published by the Penguin Group
Penguin Books Ltd, 27 Wrights Lane, London W8 5TZ, England
Penguin Books USA Inc., 375 Hudson Street, New York, New York 10014, USA
Penguin Books Australia Ltd, Ringwood, Victoria, Australia
Penguin Books Canada Ltd, 10 Alcorn Avenue, Toronto, Ontario, Canada M4V 3B2
Penguin Books (NZ) Ltd, 182–190 Wairau Road, Auckland 10, New Zealand

Penguin Books Ltd, Registered Offices: Harmondsworth, Middlesex, England

First published by Macmillan and Co. Ltd 1912
Published in Puffin Books 1988
Reissued in this edition 1994
5 7 9 10 8 6

Filmset by Datix International Limited, Bungay, Suffolk
Printed in England by Clays Ltd, St Ives plc
Set in 12/15 pt Monophoto Plantin

Contents

THE CAT-HOOD OF MAURICE

To have your hair cut is not painful, nor does it hurt to have your whiskers trimmed. But round wooden shoes, shaped like bowls, are not comfortable wear, however much it may amuse the onlooker to see you try to walk in them. If you have a nice fur coat like a company promoter's, it is most annoying to be made to swim in it. And if you had a tail, surely it would be solely your own affair; that anyone should tie a tin can to it would strike you as an unwarrantable impertinence – to say the least.

Yet it is difficult for an outsider to see these things from the point of view of both the persons concerned. To Maurice, scissors in hand, alive and earnest to snip, it seemed the most natural thing in the world to shorten the stiff whiskers of Lord Hugh Cecil by a generous inch. He did not understand how useful those whiskers were to Lord Hugh, both in sport and in the more serious business of getting a living. Also it amused Maurice to throw Lord Hugh into ponds, though Lord Hugh only once permitted this liberty. To put walnuts on Lord Hugh's feet and then to watch him walk on ice was, in Maurice's opinion, as good as a play. Lord Hugh was a very favourite cat, but Maurice was discreet, and Lord Hugh, except under violent suffering, was at that time anyhow, dumb.

But the empty sardine-tin attached to Lord Hugh's tail and hind legs – this had a voice, and, rattling against stairs, banisters, and the legs of stricken furniture, it cried aloud for vengeance. Lord Hugh, suffering violently, added his voice, and this time the family heard. There was a chase, a chorus of 'Poor pussy!' and 'Pussy, then!' and the tail and the tin and Lord Hugh were caught under Jane's bed. The tail and the tin acquiesced in their rescue. Lord Hugh did not. He fought, scratched, and bit. Jane carried the scars of that rescue for many a long week.

When all was calm Maurice was sought and, after some little natural delay, found – in the boot-cupboard.

'Oh, Maurice!' his mother almost sobbed, 'how *can* you? What will your father say?'

Maurice thought he knew what his father would do.

'Don't you know,' the mother went on, 'how wrong it is to be cruel?'

'I didn't mean to be cruel,' Maurice said. And, what is more, he spoke the truth. All the unwelcome attentions he had showered on Lord Hugh had not been exactly intended to hurt that stout veteran – only it was interesting to see what a cat would do if you threw it in the water, or cut its whiskers, or tied things to its tail.

'Oh, but you must have meant to be cruel,' said mother, 'and you will have to be punished.'

'I wish I hadn't,' said Maurice, from the heart.

'So do I,' said his mother, with a sigh; 'but it isn't the first time; you know you tied Lord Hugh up in a bag with the hedgehog only last Tuesday week. You'd better go to your room and think it over. I shall have to tell your father directly he comes home.'

Maurice went to his room and thought it over. And the more he thought the more he hated Lord Hugh. Why couldn't the beastly cat have held his tongue and sat still? That, at the time, would have been a disappointment, but now Maurice wished it had happened. He sat on the edge of his bed and savagely kicked the edge of the green Kidderminster carpet, and hated the cat.

He hadn't meant to be cruel; he was sure he hadn't; he wouldn't have pinched the cat's feet or squeezed its tail in the door, or pulled its whiskers, or poured hot water on it. He felt himself ill-used, and knew that he would feel still more so after the inevitable interview with his father.

But that interview did not take the immediately painful form expected by Maurice. His father did *not* say, 'Now I will show you what it feels like to be hurt.' Maurice had braced himself for that, and was looking beyond it to the calm of forgiveness which should follow the storm in which he should so unwillingly take part. No; his father was already calm and reasonable – with a dreadful calm, a terrifying reason.

'Look here, my boy,' he said. 'This cruelty to dumb animals must be checked – severely checked.'

'I didn't mean to be cruel,' said Maurice.

'Evil,' said Mr Basingstoke, for such was Maurice's surname, 'is wrought by want of thought as well as want of heart. What about your putting the hen in the oven?'

'You know,' said Maurice, pale but determined, 'you *know* I only wanted to help her to get her eggs hatched quickly. It says in *Fowls for Food and Fancy* that heat hatches eggs.'

'But she hadn't any eggs,' said Mr Basingstoke.

'But she soon would have,' urged Maurice. 'I thought a stitch in time . . .'

'That,' said his father, 'is the sort of thing that you must learn not to think.'

'I'll try,' said Maurice, miserably hoping for the best.

'I intend that you shall,' said Mr Basingstoke. 'This afternoon you go to Dr Strongitharm's for the remaining week of term. If I find any more cruelty taking place during the holidays you will go there permanently. You can go and get ready.'

'Oh, father, *please* not,' was all Maurice found to say.

'I'm sorry, my boy,' said his father, much more kindly; 'it's all for your own good, and it's as painful to me as it is to you – remember that. The cab will be here at four. Go and put your things together, and Jane shall pack for you.'

So the box was packed. Mabel, Maurice's kiddy sister, cried over everything as it was put in. It was a very wet day.

'If it had been any school but old Strong's,' she sobbed.

She and her brother knew that school well: its windows, dulled with wire blinds, its big alarm bell, the high walls of its grounds, bristling with spikes, the iron gates, always locked, through which gloomy boys, imprisoned, scowled on a free world. Dr Strongitharm's was a school 'for backward and difficult boys'. Need I say more?

Well, there was no help for it. The box was packed, the cab was at the door. The farewells had been said. Maurice determined that he wouldn't cry and he didn't, which gave him the one touch of pride and joy that such a scene could yield. Then at the last moment, just as father had one leg in the cab, the Taxes called. Father went back into the house to write a cheque. Mother and Mabel had retired in tears. Maurice used the reprieve to go back after his postage-stamp album. Already he was planning how to impress the other boys at old Strong's, and his was really a very fair collection. He ran up into the schoolroom, expecting to find it empty. But someone was there: Lord Hugh, in the very middle of the ink-stained tablecloth.

'You brute,' said Maurice; 'you know jolly well I'm going away, or you wouldn't be here.' And, indeed, the room had never, somehow, been a favourite of Lord Hugh's.

'Meaow,' said Lord Hugh.

'Mew!' said Maurice, with scorn. 'That's what you always say. All that fuss about a jolly little sardine-tin. Anyone would have thought you'd be only too glad to have it to play with. I wonder how you'd like being a boy? Lickings, and lessons, and impots, and sent back from breakfast to wash your ears. You wash yours anywhere – I wonder what they'd say to me if I washed my ears on the drawing-room hearthrug.'

'Meaow,' said Lord Hugh, and washed an ear, as though he were showing off.

'Mew,' said Maurice again, 'that's all you can say.'

'Oh, no, it isn't,' said Lord Hugh, and stopped his ear-washing.

'I say!' said Maurice in awestruck tones.

'If you think cats have such a jolly time,' said Lord Hugh, 'why not *be* a cat?'

'I would if I could,' said Maurice, 'and fight you –'

'Thank you,' said Lord Hugh.

'But I can't,' said Maurice.

'Oh, yes, you can,' said Lord Hugh. 'You've only got to say the word.'

'What word?'

Lord Hugh told him the word; but I will not

tell you, for fear you should say it by accident and then be sorry.

'And if I say that, I shall turn into a cat?'

'Of course,' said the cat.

'Oh, yes, I see,' said Maurice. 'But I'm not taking any, thanks. I don't want to be a cat for always.'

'You needn't,' said Lord Hugh. 'You've only got to get someone to say to you, "Please leave off being a cat and be Maurice again," and there you are.'

Maurice thought of Dr Strongitharm's. He also thought of the horror of his father when he should find Maurice gone, vanished, not to be traced. 'He'll be sorry, then,' Maurice told himself, and to the cat he said, suddenly:

'Right – I'll do it. What's the word, again?'

'. . . ,' said the cat.

'. . . ,' said Maurice; and suddenly the table shot up to the height of a house, the walls to the height of tenement buildings, the pattern on the carpet became enormous, and Maurice found himself on all fours. He tried to stand up on his feet, but his shoulders were oddly heavy. He could only rear himself upright for a moment, and then fell heavily on his hands. He looked down at them; they seemed to have grown shorter and fatter, and were encased in black fur gloves. He felt a desire to walk on all fours – tried it – did it. It was very odd – the movement of the arms straight from the shoulder, more like the movement of the piston of an engine than anything Maurice could think of at that moment.

'I am asleep,' said Maurice – 'I am dreaming this. I am dreaming I am a cat. I hope I dreamed that about the sardine-tin and Lord Hugh's tail, and Dr Strong's.'

'You didn't,' said a voice he knew and yet didn't know, 'and you aren't dreaming this.'

'Yes, I am,' said Maurice; 'and now I'm going to dream that I fight that beastly black cat, and give him the best licking he ever had in his life. Come on, Lord Hugh.'

A loud laugh answered him.

'Excuse my smiling,' said the voice he knew and didn't know, 'but don't you see – you *are* Lord Hugh!'

A great hand picked Maurice up from the floor and held him in the air. He felt the position to be not only undignified but unsafe, and gave himself a shake of mingled relief and resentment when the hand set him down on the inky table-cloth.

'You are Lord Hugh now, my dear Maurice,' said the voice, and a huge face came quite close to his. It was his own face, as it would have seemed through a magnifying glass. And the voice – oh, horror! – the voice was his own voice – Maurice Basingstoke's voice. Maurice shrank from the voice, and he would have liked to claw the face, but he had had no practice.

'You are Lord Hugh,' the voice repeated, 'and I am Maurice. I like being Maurice. I am so large and strong. I could drown you in the water-butt, my poor cat – oh, so easily. No, don't spit and swear. It's bad manners – even in a cat.'

'Maurice!' shouted Mr Basingstoke from between the door and the cab.

Maurice, from habit, leaped towards the door.

'It's no use *your* going,' said the thing that looked like a giant reflection of Maurice; 'it's *me* he wants.'

'But I didn't agree to your being me.'

'That's poetry, even if it isn't grammar,' said the thing that looked like Maurice. 'Why, my good cat, don't you see that if you are I, I must be you? Otherwise we should interfere with time and space, upset the balance of power, and as likely as not destroy the solar system. Oh, yes – I'm you, right enough, and shall be, till someone tells you to change from Lord Hugh into Maurice. And now you've got to find someone to do it.'

('Maurice!' thundered the voice of Mr Basingstoke.)

'That'll be easy enough,' said Maurice.

'Think so?' said the other.

'But I shan't try yet. I want to have some fun first. I shall catch heaps of mice!'

'Think so? You forget that your whiskers are cut off – Maurice cut them. Without whiskers, how can you judge of the width of the places you go through? Take care you don't get stuck in a hole that you can't get out of or go in through, my good cat.'

'Don't call me a cat,' said Maurice, and felt that his tail was growing thick and angry.

'You *are* a cat, you know – and that little bit of temper that I see in your tail reminds me –'

Maurice felt himself gripped round the middle, abruptly lifted, and carried swiftly through the air. The quickness of the movement made him giddy. The light went so quickly past him that it might as well have been darkness. He saw nothing, felt nothing, except a sort of long sea-sickness, and then suddenly he was not being moved. He could see now. He could feel. He was being held tight in a sort of vice – a vice covered with chequered cloth. It looked like the pattern, very much ex-aggerated, of his school knickerbockers. It *was*. He was being held between the hard, relentless knees of that creature that had once been Lord Hugh, and to whose tail he had tied a sardine-tin. Now *he* was Lord Hugh, and something was being tied to *his* tail. Something mysterious, terrible. Very well, he would show that he was not afraid of anything that could be attached to tails. The string rubbed his fur the wrong way – it was that that annoyed him, not the string itself; and as for what was at the end of the string, what *could* that matter to any sensible cat? Maurice was quite decided that he was – and would keep on being – a sensible cat.

The string, however, and the uncomfortable, tight position between those chequered knees – something or other was getting on his nerves.

'Maurice!' shouted his father below, and the be-catted Maurice bounded between the knees of the creature that wore his clothes and his looks.

'Coming, father,' this thing called, and sped away, leaving Maurice on the servant's bed – under which Lord Hugh had taken refuge, with his tin can, so short and yet so long a time ago. The stairs re-echoed to the loud boots which Maurice had never before thought loud; he had often, indeed, wondered that anyone could object to them. He wondered now no longer.

He heard the front door slam. That thing had gone to Dr Strongitharm's. That was one comfort. Lord Hugh was a boy now; he would know what it was to be a boy. He, Maurice, was a cat, and he meant to taste fully all catty pleasure, from milk to mice. Meanwhile he was without mice or milk, and, unaccustomed as he was to a tail, he could not but feel that all was not right with his own. There was a feeling of weight, a feeling of discomfort, of positive terror. If he should move, what would that thing that was tied to his tail do? Rattle, of course. Oh, but he could not bear it if that thing rattled. Nonsense; it was only a sardine-tin. Yes, Maurice knew that. But all the same – if it did rattle! He moved his tail the least little soft inch. No sound. Perhaps really there wasn't anything tied to his tail. But he couldn't be sure unless he moved. But if he moved the thing would rattle, and if it rattled Maurice felt sure that he would expire or go mad. A mad cat. What a dreadful thing to be! Yet he couldn't sit on that bed for ever, waiting, waiting, waiting for the dreadful thing to happen.

'Oh, dear,' sighed Maurice the cat. 'I never knew what people meant by "afraid" before.'

His cat-heart was beating heavily against his furry side. His limbs were getting cramped – he must move. He did. And instantly the awful thing happened. The sardine-tin touched the iron of the bed-foot. It rattled.

'Oh, I can't bear it, I can't,' cried poor Maurice, in a heartrending meaow that echoed through the house. He leaped from the bed and tore through the door and down the stairs, and behind him came the most terrible thing in the world. People might call it a sardine-tin, but he knew better. It was the soul of all the fear that ever had been or ever could be. *It rattled.*

Maurice who was a cat flew down the stairs; down, down – the rattling horror followed. Oh, horrible! Down, down! At the foot of the stairs the horror, caught by something – a banister – a stair-rod – stopped. The string on Maurice's tail tightened, his tail was jerked, he was stopped. But the noise had stopped too. Maurice lay only just alive at the foot of the stairs.

It was Mabel who untied the string and soothed his terrors with strokings and tender love-words. Maurice was surprised to find what a nice little girl his sister really was.

'I'll never tease you again,' he tried to say,

softly – but that was not what he said. What he said was 'Purrrr'.

'Dear pussy, nice poor pussy, then,' said Mabel, and she hid away the sardine-tin and did not tell anyone. This seemed unjust to Maurice until he remembered that, of course, Mabel thought that he was really Lord Hugh, and that the person who had tied the tin to his tail was her brother Maurice. Then he was half grateful. She carried him down, in soft, safe arms, to the kitchen, and asked cook to give him some milk.

'Tell me to change back into Maurice,' said Maurice who was quite worn out by his cattish experiences. But no one heard him. What they heard was, 'Meaow – Meaow – Meeeaow!'

Then Maurice saw how he had been tricked. He could be changed back into a boy as soon as anyone said to him, 'Leave off being a cat and be Maurice again,' but his tongue had no longer the power to ask anyone to say it.

He did not sleep well that night. For one thing he was not accustomed to sleeping on the kitchen hearthrug, and the blackbeetles were too many and too cordial. He was glad when cook came down and turned him out into the garden, where the October frost still lay white on the yellowed stalks of sunflowers and nasturtiums. He took a walk, climbed a tree, failed to catch a bird, and felt better. He began also to feel hungry. A delicious scent came stealing out of the back kitchen door. Oh, joy, there were to be herrings for breakfast! Maurice hastened in and took his place on his usual chair.

His mother said, 'Down, puss,' and gently tilted the chair so that Maurice fell off it. Then the family had herrings. Maurice said, 'You might give me some,' and he said it so often that his father, who, of course, heard only mewings, said:

'For goodness' sake put that cat out of the room.'

Maurice breakfasted later, in the dust-bin, on herring heads.

But he kept himself up with a new and splendid idea. They would give him milk presently, and then they should see.

He spent the afternoon sitting on the sofa in the dining-room, listening to the conversation of his father and mother. It is said that listeners never hear any good of themselves. Maurice heard so much that he was surprised and humbled. He heard his father say that he was a fine, plucky little chap, but he needed a severe lesson, and Dr Strongitharm was the man to give it to him. He heard his mother say things that made his heart throb in his throat and the tears prick behind those green cat-eyes of his. He had always thought his parents a little bit unjust. Now they did him so much more than justice that he felt quite small and mean inside his cat-skin.

'He's a dear, good, affectionate boy,' said mother. 'It's only his high spirits. Don't you think, darling, perhaps you were a little hard on him?'

'It was for his own good,' said father.

'Of course,' said mother; 'but I can't bear to think of him at that dreadful school.'

'Well –' father was beginning, when Jane came in with the tea-things on a clattering tray, whose sound made Maurice tremble in every leg. Father and mother began to talk about the weather.

Maurice felt very affectionately to both his parents. The natural way of showing this was to jump on to the sideboard and thence on to his father's shoulders. He landed there on his four padded feet, light as a feather, but father was not pleased.

'Bother the cat!' he cried. 'Jane, put it out of the room.'

Maurice was put out. His great idea, which was to be carried out with milk, would certainly not be carried out in the dining-room. He sought the kitchen, and, seeing a milk-can on the window-ledge, jumped up beside the can and patted it as he had seen Lord Hugh do.

'My!' said a friend of Jane's who happened to be there, 'ain't that cat clever – a perfect moral, I call her.'

'He's nothing to boast of this time,' said cook. 'I will say for Lord Hugh he's not often taken in with an empty can.'

This was naturally mortifying for Maurice, but

he pretended not to hear, and jumped from the window to the tea-table and patted the milk-jug.

'Come,' said the cook, 'that's more like it,' and she poured him out a full saucer and set it on the floor.

Now was the chance Maurice had longed for. Now he could carry out that idea of his. He was very thirsty, for he had had nothing since that delicious breakfast in the dust-bin. But not for worlds would he have drunk the milk. No. He carefully dipped his right paw in it, for his idea was to make letters with it on the kitchen oil-cloth. He meant to write: 'Please tell me to leave off being a cat and be Maurice again,' but he found his paw a very clumsy pen, and he had to rub out the first 'P' because it only looked like an accident. Then he tried again and actually did make a 'P' that any fair-minded person could have read quite easily.

'I wish they'd notice,' he said, and before he got the 'l' written they did notice.

'Drat the cat,' said cook; 'look how he's messing the floor up.'

And she took away the milk.

Maurice put pride aside and mewed to have the milk put down again. But he did not get it.

Very weary, very thirsty, and very tired of being Lord Hugh, he presently found his way to the schoolroom, where Mabel with patient toil was doing her home-lessons. She took him on her lap and stroked him while she learned her French verbs. He felt that he was growing very fond of her. People were quite right to be kind to dumb animals. Presently she had to stop stroking him and do a map. And after that she kissed him and put him down and went away. All the time she had been doing the map, Maurice had had but one thought: *Ink!*

The moment the door had closed behind her – how sensible people were who closed doors gently – he stood up in her chair with one paw on the map and the other on the ink. Unfortunately, the inkstand top was made to dip pens in, and not to dip paws. But Maurice was desperate. He deliberately upset the ink – most of it rolled over the table-cloth and fell pattering on the carpet, but with what was left he wrote quite plainly, across the map:

> 'Please tell Lord Hugh
> to stop being
> a cat and be Mau
> rice again.'

'There!' he said; 'they can't make any mistake about that.' They didn't. But they made a mistake about who had done it, and Mabel was deprived of jam with her supper bread.

Her assurance that some naughty boy must have come through the window and done it while she was not there convinced nobody, and, indeed, the window was shut and bolted.

Maurice, wild with indignation, did not mend matters by seizing the opportunity of a few minutes' solitude to write:

> 'It was not Mabel
> it was Maur
> ice I mean Lord Hugh,'

because when that was seen Mabel was instantly sent to bed.

'It's not fair!' cried Maurice.

'My dear,' said Maurice's father, 'if that cat goes on mewing to this extent you'll have to get rid of it.'

Maurice said not another word. It was bad enough to be a cat, but to be a cat that was 'got rid of'! He knew how people got rid of cats. In a stricken silence he left the room and slunk up the stairs – he dared not mew again, even at the door of Mabel's room. But when Jane went in to put Mabel's light out Maurice crept in too, and in the dark tried with stifled mews and purrs to explain to Mabel how sorry he was. Mabel stroked him and he went to sleep, his last waking thought amazement at the blindness that had once made him call her a silly little kid.

If you have ever been a cat you will understand something of what Maurice endured during the dreadful days that followed. If you have not, I can never make you understand fully. There was the affair of the fishmonger's tray balanced on the wall by the back door – the delicious curled-up whiting; Maurice knew as well as you do that one mustn't steal fish out of other's trays, but the cat that he was didn't know. There was an inward struggle – and Maurice was beaten by the cat-nature. Later he was beaten by the cook.

Then there was that very painful incident with the butcher's dog, the flight across gardens, the safety of the plum tree gained only just in time.

And, worst of all, despair took hold of him, for he saw that nothing he could do would make anyone say those simple words that would release him. He had hoped that Mabel might at last be made to understand, but the ink had failed him; she did not understand his subdued mewings, and when he got the cardboard letters and made the same sentence with them Mabel only thought it was that naughty boy who came through locked windows. Somehow he could not spell before anyone – his nerves were not what they had been. His brain now gave him no new ideas. He felt that he was really growing like a cat in his mind. His interest in his meals grew beyond even what it had been when they were a schoolboy's meals. He hunted mice with growing enthusiasm, though the loss of his whiskers to measure narrow places with made hunting difficult.

He grew expert in bird-stalking, and often got quite near to a bird before it flew away, laughing at him. But all the time, in his heart, he was very, very miserable. And so the week went by.

Maurice in his cat shape dreaded more and more the time when Lord Hugh in the boy shape should come back from Dr Strongitharm's. He knew – who better? – exactly the kind of things boys do to cats, and he trembled to the end of his handsome half-Persian tail.

And then the boy came home from Dr Strongitharm's, and at the first sound of his boots in the hall Maurice in the cat's body fled with silent haste to hide in the boot-cupboard.

Here, ten minutes later, the boy that had come back from Dr Strongitharm's found him.

Maurice fluffed up his tail and unsheathed his claws. Whatever this boy was going to do to him Maurice meant to resist, and his resistance should hurt the boy as much as possible. I am sorry to say Maurice swore softly among the boots, but cat-swearing is not really wrong.

'Come out, you old duffer,' said Lord Hugh in the boy shape of Maurice. 'I'm not going to hurt you.'

'I'll see to that,' said Maurice, backing into the corner, all teeth and claws.

'Oh, I've had such a time!' said Lord Hugh. 'It's no use, you know, old chap; I can see where you are by your green eyes. My word, they do shine. I've been caned and shut up in a dark room and given thousands of lines to write out.'

'I've been beaten, too, if you come to that,' mewed Maurice. 'Besides the butcher's dog.'

It was an intense relief to speak to someone who could understand his mews.

'Well, I suppose it's Pax for the future,' said Lord Hugh; 'if you won't come out, you won't. Please leave off being a cat and be Maurice again.'

And instantly Maurice, amid a heap of goloshes and old tennis bats, felt with a swelling heart that he was no longer a cat. No more of those undignified four legs, those tiresome pointed ears, so difficult to wash, that furry coat, that contemptible tail, and that terrible inability to express all one's feelings in two words – 'mew' and 'purr'.

He scrambled out of the cupboard, and the boots and goloshes fell off him like spray off a bather.

He stood upright in those very chequered knickerbockers that were so terrible when their knees held one vice-like, while things were tied to one's tail. He was face to face with another boy, exactly like himself.

'*You* haven't changed, then – but there can't be two Maurices.'

'There shan't be; not if I know it,' said the other boy; 'a boy's life a dog's life. Quick, before anyone comes.'

'Quick what?' asked Maurice.

'Why, tell me to leave off being a boy, and to be Lord Hugh Cecil again.'

Maurice told him at once. And at once the boy was gone, and there was Lord Hugh in his own shape, purring politely, yet with a watchful eye on Maurice's movements.

'Oh, you needn't be afraid, old chap. It's Pax

right enough,' Maurice murmured in the ear of Lord Hugh. And Lord Hugh, arching his back under Maurice's stroking hand, replied with a purrrr-meaow that spoke volumes.

'Oh, Maurice, here you are. It *is* nice of you to be nice to Lord Hugh, when it was because of him you –'

'He's a good old chap,' said Maurice, carelessly. 'And you're not half a bad old girl. See?'

Mabel almost wept for joy at this magnificent compliment, and Lord Hugh himself took on a more happy and confident air.

Please dismiss any fears which you may entertain that after this Maurice became a model boy. He didn't. But he was much nicer than before. The conversation which he overheard when he was a cat makes him more patient with his father and mother. And he is almost always nice to Mabel, for he cannot forget all that she was to him when he wore the shape of Lord Hugh. His father attributes all the improvement in his son's character to that week at Dr Strongitharm's – which, as you know, Maurice never had. Lord Hugh's character is unchanged. Cats learn slowly and with difficulty.

Only Maurice and Lord Hugh know the truth – Maurice has never told it to anyone except me, and Lord Hugh is a very reserved cat. He never at any time had that free flow of mew which distinguished and endangered the cat-hood of Maurice.

2

THE MIXED MINE

The ship was first sighted off Dungeness. She was labouring heavily. Her paint was peculiar and her rig outlandish. She looked like a golden ship out of a painted picture.

'Blessed if I ever see such a rig – nor such lines neither,' old Hawkhurst said.

It was a late afternoon, wild and grey. Slate-coloured clouds drove across the sky like flocks of hurried camels. The waves were purple and blue, and in the west a streak of unnatural-looking green light was all that stood for the splendours of sunset.

'She do be a rum 'un,' said young Benenden, who had strolled along the beach with the glasses the gentleman gave him for saving the little boy from drowning. 'Don't know as I ever see another just like her.'

'I'd give half a dollar to any chap as can tell me where she hails from – and what port it is where they has ships o' that cut,' said middle-aged Haversham to the group that had now gathered.

'George!' exclaimed young Benenden from under his field-glasses, 'she's going.' And she went. Her bow went down suddenly and she stood stern up in the water – like a duck after rain. Then quite slowly, with no unseemly hurry, but with no moment's change of what seemed to be her fixed purpose, the ship sank and the grey rolling waves wiped out the place where she had been.

Now I hope you will not expect me to tell you anything more about this ship – because there is nothing more to tell. What country she came from, what port she was bound for, what cargo she carried, and what kind of tongue her crew spoke – all these things are dead secrets. And a dead secret is a secret that nobody knows. No other secrets are dead secrets. Even I do not know this one, or I would tell you at once. For I, at least, have no secrets from you.

When ships go down off Dungeness, things from them have a way of being washed up on the sands of that bay which curves from Dungeness to Folkestone, where the sea has bitten a piece out of the land – just such a half-moon-shaped piece as you bite out of a slice of bread-and-butter. Bits of wood tangled with ropes – broken furniture – ships' biscuits in barrels and kegs that have held brandy – seamen's chests – and sometimes sadder things that we will not talk about just now.

Now, if you live by the sea and are grown-up you know that if you find anything on the seashore (I don't mean starfish or razor-shells or jellyfish and sea-mice, but anything out of a ship that you would really like to keep) your duty is to take it up to the coast-guard and say, 'Please, I've found this.' Then the coast-guard will send it to the proper authority, and one of these days you'll get a reward of one-third of the value of whatever it was that you picked up. But two-thirds of the value of anything, or even three-thirds of its value, is not at all the same thing as the thing itself – if it happened to be the kind of thing you want. But if you are not grown-up and do not live by the sea, but in a nice little villa in a nice little suburb, where all the furniture is new and the servants wear white aprons and white caps with long strings in the afternoon, then you won't know anything about your duty, and if you find anything by the sea you'll think that findings are keepings.

Edward was not grown-up – and he kept everything he found, including sea-mice, till the landlady of the lodgings where his aunt was threw his collection into the pig-pail.

Being a quiet and persevering little boy he did not cry or complain, but having meekly followed his treasures to their long home – the pig was six feet from nose to tail, and ate the dead sea-mouse as easily and happily as your father eats an oyster – he started out to make a new collection.

And the first thing he found was an oyster-shell that was pink and green and blue inside, and the second was an old boot – very old indeed – and the third was *it*.

It was a square case of old leather embossed with odd little figures of men and animals and words that Edward could not read. It was oblong and had no key, but a sort of leather hasp, and was curiously knotted with string – rather like a boot-lace. And Edward opened it. There were several things inside: queer-looking instruments, some rather like those in the little box of mathematical instruments that he had had as a prize at school, and some like nothing he had ever seen before. And in a deep groove of the russet soaked velvet lining lay a neat little brass telescope.

T-squares and set-squares and so forth are of little use on a sandy shore. But you can always look through a telescope.

Edward picked it out and put it to his eye, and tried to see through it a little tug that was sturdily puffing up the channel. He failed to find the tug, and found himself gazing at a little cloud on the horizon. As he looked it grew larger and darker, and presently a spot of rain fell on his nose. He rubbed it off – on his jersey sleeve, I am sorry to say, and not on his handkerchief. Then he looked through the glass again; but he found he needed both hands to keep it steady, so he set down the box with the other instruments on the sand at his feet and put the glass to his eye again.

He never saw the box again. For in his unpractised efforts to cover the tug with his glass he found himself looking at the shore instead of at the sea, and the shore looked so odd that he could not make up his mind to stop looking at it.

He had thought it was a sandy shore, but almost at once he saw that it was not sand but fine shingle, and the discovery of this mistake surprised him so much that he kept on looking at the shingle through the little telescope, which showed it quite plainly. And as he looked the shingle grew coarser; it was stones now – quite decent-sized stones, large stones, enormous stones.

Something hard pressed against his foot, and he lowered the glass.

He was surrounded by big stones, and they all seemed to be moving; some were tumbling off others that lay in heaps below them, and others were rolling away from the beach in every direction. And the place where he had put down the box was covered with great stones which he could not move.

Edward was very much upset. He had never been accustomed to great stones that moved about when no one was touching them, and he looked round for someone to ask how it had happened.

The only person in sight was another boy in a blue jersey with red letters on its chest.

'Hi!' said Edward, and the boy also said 'Hi!'

'Come along here,' said Edward, 'and I'll show you something.'

'Right-o!' the boy remarked, and came.

The boy was staying at the camp where the white tents were below the Grand Redoubt. His home was quite unlike Edward's, though he also lived with his aunt. The boy's home was very dirty and very small, and nothing in it was ever in its right place. There was no furniture to speak of. The servants did not wear white caps with long streamers, because there were no servants. His uncle was a dock labourer and his aunt went out washing. But he had felt just the same pleasure in being shown things that Edward or you or I might have felt, and he went climbing over the big stones to where Edward stood waiting for him in a sort of pit among the stones with the little telescope in his hand.

'I say,' said Edward, 'did you see anyone move these stones?'

'I ain't only just come up on to the sea-wall,' said the boy, who was called Gustus.

'They all came round me,' said Edward, rather pale. 'I didn't see anyone shoving them.'

'Who're you a-kiddin' of?' the boy inquired.

'But I *did*,' said Edward, 'honour bright I did. I was just taking a squint through this little telescope I've found – and they came rolling up to me.'

'Let's see what you found,' said Gustus, and Edward gave him the glass. He directed it with inexpert fingers to the sea-wall, so little trodden that on it the grass grows, and the sea-pinks, and even convolvulus and mock-strawberry.

'Oh, look!' cried Edward, very loud. 'Look at the grass!'

Gustus let the glass fall to long arm's length and said 'Krikey!'

The grass and flowers on the sea-wall had grown a foot and a half – quite tropical they looked.

'Well?' said Edward.

'What's the matter wiv everyfink?' said Gustus. 'We must both be a bit balmy, seems ter me.'

'What's balmy?' asked Edward.

'Off your chump – looney – like what you and me is,' said Gustus. 'First I sees things, then I sees you.'

'It was only fancy, I expect,' said Edward. 'I expect the grass on the sea-wall was always like that, really.'

'Let's have a look through your spy-glass at that little barge,' said Gustus, still holding the glass. 'Come on outer these 'ere paving-stones.'

'There was a box,' said Edward, 'a box I found with lots of jolly things in it. I laid it down somewhere – and . . .'

'Ain't that it over there?' Gustus asked, and levelled the glass at a dark object a hundred yards away. 'No; it's only an old boot. I say, this is a fine spy-glass. It does make things come big.'

'That's not it. I'm certain I put it down somewhere just here. Oh, *don't*!'

He snatched the glass from Gustus.

'Look!' he said, 'look!' and pointed.

A hundred yards away stood a boot about as big as the bath you see Marat in at Madame Tussaud's.

'S'welp me,' said Gustus, 'we're asleep, both of us, and a-dreaming as things grow while we look at them.'

'But we're not dreaming,' Edward objected. 'You let me pinch you and you'll see.'

'No fun in that,' said Gustus. 'Tell you what – it's the spy-glass – that's what it is. Ever see any conjuring? I see a chap at the Mile End Empire what made things turn into things like winking. It's the spy-glass, that's what it is.'

'It can't be,' said the little boy who lived in a villa.

'But it *is*,' said the little boy who lived in a slum. 'Teacher says there ain't no bounds to the wonders of science. Blest if this ain't one of 'em.'

'Let me look,' said Edward.

'All right; only you mark me. Whatever you sets eyes on'll grow and grow – like the flower-tree the conjurer had under the wipe. Don't you look at *me*, that's all. Hold on; I'll put something up for you to look at – a mark like – something as doesn't matter.'

He fumbled in his pocket and brought out a boot-lace.

'I hold this up,' he said, 'and you look.'

Next moment he had dropped the boot-lace, which, swollen as it was with the magic of the glass, lay like a snake on the stone at his feet.

So the glass *was* a magic glass, as, of course, you know already.

'My!' said Gustus, 'wouldn't I like to look at my victuals through that there!'

Thus we find Edward, of the villa – and through him Gustus, of the slum – in possession of a unique instrument of magic. What could they do with it?

This was the question which they talked over every time they met, and they met continually. Edward's aunt, who at home watched him as cats watch mice, rashly believed that at the seaside there was no mischief for a boy to get into. And the gentleman who commanded the tented camp believed in the ennobling effects of liberty.

After the boot, neither had dared to look at anything through the telescope – and so they looked *at* it, and polished it on their sleeves till it shone again.

Both were agreed that it would be a fine thing to get some money and look at it, so that it would grow big. But Gustus never had any pocket-money, and Edward had had his confiscated to pay for a window he had not intended to break.

Gustus felt certain that someone would find out about the spy-glass and take it away from them. His experience was that anything you happened to like was always taken away. Edward knew that his aunt would want to take the telescope away to 'take care of' for him. This had already happened with the carved chessmen that his father had sent him from India.

'I been thinking,' said Gustus, on the third day. 'When I'm a man I'm a-going to be a burglar. You has to use your headpiece in that trade, I tell you. So I don't think thinking's swipes, like some blokes do. And I think p'raps it don't turn everything big. An' if we could find out what it don't turn big we could see what we wanted to turn big or what it didn't turn big, and then it wouldn't turn anything big except what we wanted it to. See?'

Edward did not see; and I don't suppose you do, either.

So Gustus went on to explain that teacher had told him there were some substances impervious to light, and some to cold, and so on and so forth, and that what they wanted was a substance that should be impervious to the magic effects of the spy-glass.

'So if we get a tanner and set it on a plate and squint at it it'll get bigger – but so'll the plate. And we don't want to litter the place up with plates the bigness of cartwheels. But if the plate didn't get big we could look at the tanner till it covered the plate, and then go on looking and looking and looking and see nothing but the tanner till it was as big as a circus. See?'

This time Edward did see. But they got no further, because it was time to go to the circus. There was a circus at Dymchurch just then, and that was what made Gustus think of the sixpence growing to that size.

It was a very nice circus, and all the boys from the camp went to it – also Edward, who managed to scramble over and wriggle under benches till he was sitting near his friend.

It was the size of the elephant that did it. Edward had not seen an elephant before, and when he saw it, instead of saying, 'What a size he is!' as everybody else did, he said to himself, 'What a size I could make him!' and pulled out the spy-glass, and by a miracle of good luck or bad got it levelled at the elephant as it went by. He turned the glass slowly – as it went out – and the elephant only just got out in time. Another moment and it would have been too big to get through the door. The audience cheered madly. They thought it was a clever trick; and so it would have been, very clever.

'You silly cuckoo,' said Gustus, bitterly, 'now you've turned that great thing loose on the country, and how's his keeper to manage him?'

'I could make the keeper big, too.'

'Then if I was you I should just bunk out and do it.'

Edward obeyed, slipped under the canvas of the circus tent, and found himself on the yellow, trampled grass of the field among guy-ropes, orange-peel, banana-skins, and dirty paper. Far above him and everyone else towered the elephant – it was now as big as the church.

Edward pointed the glass at the man who was patting the elephant's foot – that was as far up as he could reach – and telling it to 'Come down with you!' He was very much frightened. He did not know whether you could be put in prison for making an elephant's keeper about forty times his proper size. But he felt that something must be done to control the gigantic mountain of black-lead-coloured living flesh. So he looked at the keeper through the spy-glass, and the keeper remained his normal size!

In the shock of this failure he dropped the spy-glass, picked it up, and tried once more to fix the keeper. Instead he only got a circle of black-lead-coloured elephant; and while he was trying to find the keeper, and finding nothing but more and more of the elephant, a shout startled him and he dropped the glass once more. He was a very clumsy little boy, was Edward.

'Well,' said one of the men, 'what a turn it give me! I thought Jumbo'd grown as big as a railway station, s'welp me if I didn't.'

'Now that's rum,' said another, 'so did I.'

'And he *ain't*,' said a third; 'seems to me he's a bit below his usual figure. Got a bit thin or something, ain't he?'

Edward slipped back into the tent unobserved.

'It's all right,' he whispered to his friend, 'he's gone back to his proper size, and the man didn't change at all.'

'Ho!' Gustus said slowly – 'Ho! All right. Conjuring's a rum thing. You don't never know where you are!'

'Don't you think you might as well be a conjurer as a burglar?' suggested Edward, who had had his friend's criminal future rather painfully on his mind for the last hour.

'*You* might,' said Gustus, 'not me. My people ain't dooks to set me up on any such a swell lay as conjuring. Now I'm going to think, I am. You hold your jaw and look at the 'andsome Dona a-doin' of 'er griceful bare-backed hact.'

That evening after tea Edward went, as he had been told to do, to the place on the shore where the big stones had taught him the magic of the spy-glass.

Gustus was already at the tryst.

'See here,' he said, 'I'm a-goin' to do something brave and fearless, I am, like Lord Nelson and the boy on the fire-ship. You out with that spy-glass, an' I'll let you look at *me*. Then we'll know where we are.'

'But s'pose you turn into a giant?'

'Don't care. 'Sides, I shan't. T'other bloke didn't.'

'P'raps,' said Edward, cautiously, 'it only works by the seashore.'

'Ah,' said Gustus, reproachfully, 'you've been a-trying to think, that's what you've been a-doing. What about the elephant, my emernent scientister? Now, then!'

Very much afraid, Edward pulled out the glass and looked.

And nothing happened.

'That's number one,' said Gustus, 'now, number two.'

He snatched the telescope from Edward's hand, and turned it round and looked through the other end at the great stones. Edward, standing by, saw them get smaller and smaller – turn to pebbles, to beach, to sand. When Gustus turned the glass to the giant grass and flowers on the sea-wall, they also drew back into themselves, got smaller and smaller, and presently were as they had been before ever Edward picked up the magic spy-glass.

'Now we know all about it – I *don't* think,' said Gustus. 'Tomorrow we'll have a look at that there model engine of yours that you say works.'

They did. They had a look at it through the spy-glass, and it became a quite efficient motor; of rather an odd pattern it is true, and very bumpy, but capable of quite a decent speed. They went up to the hills in it, and so odd was its design that no one who saw it ever forgot it. People talk about that rummy motor at Bonnington and Aldington to this day. They stopped often, to use the spy-glass on various objects. Trees, for instance, could be made to grow surprisingly, and there were patches of giant wheat found that year near Ashford that were never satisfactorily accounted for. Blackberries, too, could be enlarged to a most wonderful and delicious fruit. And the sudden growth of a fugitive toffee-drop found in Edward's pocket and placed on the hand was a happy surprise. When you scraped the pocket dirt off the outside you had a pound of delicious toffee. Not so happy was the incident of the earwig, which crawled into view when Edward was enlarging a wild strawberry, and had grown the size of a rat before the slow but horrified Edward gained courage to shake it off.

It was a beautiful drive. As they came home they met a woman driving a weak-looking little cow. It went by on one side of the engine and the woman went by on the other. When they were restored to each other the cow was nearly the size of a cart-horse, and the woman did not recognize it. She ran back along the road after her cow, which must, she said, have taken fright at the beastly motor. She scolded violently as she went. So the boys had to make the cow small again, when she wasn't looking.

'This is all very well,' said Gustus, 'but we've got our fortune to make, I don't think. We've got to get hold of a tanner – or a bob would be better.'

But this was not possible, because that broken window wasn't paid for, and Gustus never had any money.

'We ought to be the benefactors of the human race,' said Edward; 'make all the good things more and all the bad things less.'

And *that* was all very well – but the cow hadn't been a great success, as Gustus reminded him.

'I see I shall have to do some of my thinking,' he added.

They stopped in a quiet road close by Dymchurch; the engine was made small again, and Edward went home with it under his arm.

It was the next day that they found the shilling on the road. They could hardly believe their good luck. They went out on to the shore with it, put it on Edward's hand while Gustus looked at it with the glass, and the shilling began to grow.

'It's as big as a saucer,' said Edward, 'and it's heavy. I'll rest it on these stones. It's as big as a plate; it's as big as a tea-tray; it's as big as a cart-wheel.'

And it was.

'Now,' said Gustus, 'we'll go and borrow a cart to take it away. Come on.'

But Edward could not come on. His hand was in the hollow between the two stones, and above lay tons of silver. He could not move, and the stones couldn't move. There was nothing for it but to look at the great round lump of silver through the wrong end of the spy-glass till it got small enough for Edward to lift it. And then, unfortunately, Gustus looked a little too long, and the shilling, having gone back to its own size, went a little further – and it went to sixpenny size, and then went out altogether.

So nobody got anything by that.

And now came the time when, as was to be expected, Edward dropped the telescope in his aunt's presence. She said, 'What's that?' picked it up with quite unfair quickness, and looked through it, and through the open window at a fishing-boat, which instantly swelled to the size of a man-of-war.

'My goodness! what a strong glass!' said the aunt.

'Isn't it?' said Edward, gently taking it from her. He looked at the ship through the glass's other end till she got to her proper size again and then smaller. He just stopped in time to prevent its disappearing altogether.

'I'll take care of it for you,' said the aunt. And for the first time in their lives Edward said 'No' to his aunt.

It was a terrible moment.

Edward, quite frenzied by his own courage, turned the glass on one object after another – the furniture grew as he looked, and when he lowered the glass the aunt was pinned fast between a monster table-leg and a great chiffonier.

'There!' said Edward. 'And I shan't let you out till you say you won't take it to take care of either.'

'Oh, have it your own way,' said the aunt, faintly, and closed her eyes. When she opened them the furniture was its right size and Edward was gone. He had twinges of conscience, but the aunt never mentioned the subject again. I have reason to suppose that *she* supposed that she had had a fit of an unusual and alarming nature.

Next day the boys in the camp were to go back to their slums. Edward and Gustus parted on the seashore and Edward cried. He had never met a boy whom he liked as he liked Gustus. And Gustus himself was almost melted.

'I will say for you you're more like a man and less like a snivelling white rabbit now than what you was when I met you. Well, we ain't done nothing to speak of with that there conjuring trick of yours, but we've 'ad a right good time. So long. See you 'gain some day.'

Edward hesitated, spluttered, and still weeping flung his arms round Gustus.

'Ere, none o' that,' said Gustus, sternly. 'If you ain't man enough to know better, I am. Shake 'ands like a Briton; right about face – and part game.'

He suited the action to the word.

Edward went back to his aunt snivelling, defenceless but happy. He had never had a friend except Gustus, and now he had given Gustus the greatest treasure that he possessed.

For Edward was not such a white rabbit as he seemed. And in that last embrace he had managed to slip the little telescope into the pocket of the reefer coat which Gustus wore, ready for his journey.

It was the greatest treasure that Edward had, but it was also the greatest responsibility, so that while he felt the joy of self-sacrifice he also felt the rapture of relief. Life is full of such mixed moments.

And the holidays ended and Edward went back to his villa. Be sure he had given Gustus his home address, and begged him to write, but Gustus never did.

Presently Edward's father came home from India, and they left his aunt to her villa and went to live at a jolly little house on a sloping hill at Chiselhurst, which was Edward's father's very own. They were not rich, and Edward could not go to a very good school, and though there was enough to eat and wear, what there was was very plain. And Edward's father had been wounded, and somehow had not got a pension.

Now one night in the next summer Edward woke up in his bed with the feeling that there was someone in the room. And there was. A dark figure was squeezing itself through the window. Edward was far too frightened to scream. He simply lay and listened to his heart. It was like listening to a cheap American clock. The next moment a lantern flashed in his eyes and a masked face bent over him.

'Where does your father keep his money?' said a muffled voice.

'In the b-b-b-b-bank,' replied the wretched Edward, truthfully.

'I mean what he's got in the house.'

'In his trousers pocket,' said Edward, 'only he puts it in the dressing-table drawer at night.'

'You must go and get it,' said the burglar, for such he plainly was.

'Must I?' said Edward, wondering how he could get out of betraying his father's confidence and being branded as a criminal.

'Yes,' said the burglar in an awful voice, 'get up and go.'

'*No*,' said Edward, and he was as much surprised at his courage as you are.

'Bravo!' said the burglar, flinging off his mask. 'I see you *aren't* such a white rabbit as what I thought you.'

'It's Gustus,' said Edward. 'Oh, Gustus, I'm so glad! Oh, Gustus, I'm so sorry! I always hoped you wouldn't be a burglar. And now you are.'

'I am so,' said Gustus, with pride, 'but,' he added sadly, 'this is my first burglary.'

'Couldn't it be the last?' suggested Edward.

'That,' replied Gustus, 'depends on you.'

'I'll do anything,' said Edward, 'anything.'

'You see,' said Gustus, sitting down on the edge of the bed in a confidential attitude, with the dark lantern in one hand and the mask in the other, 'when you're as hard up as we are, there's not much of a living to be made honest. I'm sure I wonder we don't all of us turn burglars, so I do. And that glass of yours – you little beggar – you did me proper – sticking of that thing in my pocket like what you did. Well, it kept us alive last winter, that's a cert. I used to look at the victuals with it, like what I said I would. A farden's worth o' pease-pudden was a dinner for three when that glass was about, and a penn'orth o' scraps turned into a big beef-steak almost. They used to wonder how I got so much for the money. But I'm always afraid o' being found out – or of losing the blessed spy-glass – or of someone pinching it. So we got to do what I always said – make some use of it. And if I go along and nick your father's dibs we'll make our fortunes right away.'

'No,' said Edward, 'but I'll ask father.'

'Rot.' Gustus was crisp and contemptuous. 'He'd think you was off your chump, and he'd get me lagged.'

'It would be stealing,' said Edward.

'Not when you'll pay it back.'

'Yes, it would,' said Edward. 'Oh, don't ask me – I can't.'

'Then I shall,' said Gustus. 'Where's his room?'

'Oh, don't!' said Edward. 'I've got a half-sovereign of my own. I'll give you that.'

'Lawk!' said Gustus. 'Why the blue monkeys couldn't you say so? Come on.'

He pulled Edward out of bed by the leg, hurried his clothes on anyhow, and half-dragged, half-coaxed him through the window and down by the ivy and the chicken-house roof.

They stood face to face in the sloping garden and Edward's teeth chattered. Gustus caught him by his hand, and led him away.

At the other end of the shrubbery, where the rockery was, Gustus stooped and dragged out a big clinker – then another, and another. There was a hole like a big rabbit-hole. If Edward had really been a white rabbit it would just have fitted him.

'I'll go first,' said Gustus, and went, head-foremost. 'Come on,' he said, hollowly, from inside. And Edward, too, went. It was dreadful crawling into that damp hole in the dark. As his head got through the hole he saw that it led to a cave, and below him stood a dark figure. The lantern was on the ground.

'Come on,' said Gustus, 'I'll catch you if you fall.'

With a rush and a scramble Edward got in.

'It's caves,' said Gustus. 'A chap I know that goes about the country bottoming cane chairs, 'e told me about it. And I nosed about and found he lived here. So then I thought what a go. So now we'll put your half-shiner down and look at it, and we'll have a gold-mine, and you can pretend to find it.'

'Halves!' said Edward, briefly and firmly.

'You're a man,' said Gustus. 'Now, then!' He led the way through a maze of chalk caves till they came to a convenient spot, which he had marked. And now Edward emptied his pockets on the sand – he had brought all the contents of his money-box, and there was more silver than gold, and more copper than either, and more odd rubbish than there was anything else. You know what a boy's pockets are like. Stones and putty, and slate-pencils and marbles – I urge in excuse that

Edward was a very little boy – a bit of plasticine, one or two bits of wood.

'No time to sort 'em,' said Gustus, and, putting the lantern in a suitable position, he got out the glass and began to look through it at the tumbled heap.

And the heap began to grow. It grew out sideways till it touched the walls of the recess, and outwards till it touched the top of the recess, and then it slowly worked out into the big cave and came nearer and nearer to the boys. Everything grew – stones, putty, money, wood, plasticine.

Edward patted the growing mass as though it were alive and he loved it, and Gustus said:

'Here's clothes, and beef, and bread, and tea, and coffee – and baccy – and a good school, and me a engineer. I see it all a-growing and a-growing.'

'Hi – stop!' said Edward suddenly.

Gustus dropped the telescope. It rolled away into the darkness.

'Now you've done it,' said Edward.

'What?' said Gustus.

'My hand,' said Edward, 'it's fast between the rock and the gold and things. Find the glass and make it go smaller so that I can get my hand out.'

But Gustus could not find the glass. And, what is more, no one ever has found it to this day.

'It's no good,' said Gustus, at last. 'I'll go and find your father. They must come and dig you out of this precious Tom Tiddler's ground.'

'And they'll lag you if they see you. You said they would,' said Edward, not at all sure what lagging was, but sure that it was something dreadful. 'Write a letter and put it in his letter-box. They'll find it in the morning.'

'And leave you pinned by the hand all night? Likely – I *don't* think,' said Gustus.

'I'd rather,' said Edward, bravely, but his voice was weak. 'I couldn't bear you to be lagged, Gustus. I do love you so.'

'None of that,' said Gustus, sternly. 'I'll leave you the lamp; I can find my way with matches. Keep up your pecker, and never say die.'

'I won't,' said Edward, bravely. 'Oh, Gustus!'

That was how it happened that Edward's father was roused from slumbers by violent shakings from an unknown hand, while an unknown voice uttered these surprising words:

'Edward is in the gold and silver and copper mine that we've found under your garden. Come and get him out.'

When Edward's father was at last persuaded that Gustus was not a silly dream – and this took some time – he got up.

He did not believe a word that Gustus said, even when Gustus added 'S'welp me!' which he did several times.

But Edward's bed was empty – his clothes gone.

Edward's father got the gardener from next

door – with, at the suggestion of Gustus, a pick – the hole in the rockery was enlarged, and they all got in.

And when they got to the place where Edward was, there, sure enough, was Edward, pinned by the hand between a piece of wood and a piece of rock. Neither the father nor the gardener noticed any metal. Edward had fainted.

They got him out; a couple of strokes with the pick released his hand, but it was bruised and bleeding.

They all turned to go, but they had not gone twenty yards before there was a crash and a loud report like thunder, and a slow rumbling, rattling noise very dreadful to hear.

'Get out of this quick, sir,' said the gardener; 'the roof's fell in; this part of the caves ain't safe.'

Edward was very feverish and ill for several days, during which he told his father the whole story – of which his father did not believe a word. But he was kind to Gustus, because Gustus was evidently fond of Edward.

When Edward was well enough to walk in the garden his father and he found that a good deal of the shrubbery had sunk, so that the trees looked as though they were growing in a pit.

It spoiled the look of the garden, and Edward's father decided to move the trees to the other side.

When this was done the first tree uprooted showed a dark hollow below it. The man is not born who will not examine and explore a dark hollow in his own grounds. So Edward's father explored.

This is the true story of the discovery of that extraordinary vein of silver, copper, and gold which has excited so much interest in scientific and mining circles. Learned papers have been written about it, learned professors have been rude to each other about it, but no one knows how it came there except Gustus and Edward and you and me. Edward's father is quite as ignorant as any one else, but he is much richer than most of them; and, at any rate, he knows that it was Gustus who first told him of the gold-mine, and who risked being lagged – arrested by the police, that is – rather than let Edward wait till morning with his hand fast between wood and rock.

So Edward and Gustus have been to a good school, and now they are at Winchester, and presently they will be at Oxford. And when Gustus is twenty-one he will have half the money that came from the gold-mine. And then he and Edward mean to start a school of their own. And the boys who are to go to it are to be the sort of boys who go to the summer camp of the Grand Redoubt near the sea – the kind of boy that Gustus was.

So the spy-glass will do some good after all, though it *was* so unmanageable to begin with.

Perhaps it may even be found again. But I rather hope it won't. It might, really, have done much more mischief than it did – and if anyone found it, it might do more yet.

There is no moral to this story, except . . . But no – there is no moral.

3

ACCIDENTAL MAGIC; OR DON'T TELL ALL YOU KNOW

Quentin de Ward was rather a nice little boy, but he had never been with other little boys, and that made him in some ways a little different from other little boys. His father was in India, and he and his mother lived in a little house in the New Forest. The house – it was a cottage really, but even a cottage is a house, isn't it? – was very pretty and thatched and had a porch covered with honeysuckle and ivy and white roses, and straight red hollyhocks were trained to stand up in a row against the south wall of it. The two lived quite alone, and as they had no one else to talk to they talked to each other a good deal. Mrs de Ward read a great many books, and she used to tell Quentin about them afterwards. They were usually books about out of the way things, for Mrs de Ward was interested in all the things that people are not quite sure about – the things that are hidden and secret, wonderful and mysterious – the things people make discoveries about. So that when the two were having their tea on the little brick terrace in front of the hollyhocks, with the white cloth flapping in the breeze, and the wasps hovering round the jam-pot, it was no uncommon thing for Quentin to say thickly through his bread and jam:

'I say, mother, tell me some more about Atlantis.' Or, 'Mother, tell me some more about ancient Egypt and the little toy boats they made for their little boys.' Or, 'Mother, tell me about the people who think Lord Bacon wrote Shakespeare.'

And his mother always told him as much as she thought he could understand, and he always understood quite half of what she told him.

They always talked the things out thoroughly, and thus he learned to be fond of arguing, and to enjoy using his brains, just as you enjoy using your muscles in the football field or the gymnasium.

Also he came to know quite a lot of odd, out of the way things, and to have opinions of his own concerning the lost Kingdom of Atlantis, and the Man with the Iron Mask, the building of Stonehenge, the Pre-dynastic Egyptians, cuneiform writings and Assyrian sculptures, the Mexican pyramids and the shipping activities of Tyre and Sidon.

Quentin did no regular lessons, such as most boys have, but he read all sorts of books and made notes from them, in a large and straggling handwriting.

You will already have supposed that Quentin was a prig. But he wasn't, and you would have owned this if you had seen him scampering through the greenwood on his quiet New Forest pony, or setting snares for the rabbits that *would* get into the garden and eat the precious lettuces and parsley. Also he fished in the little streams that run though that lovely land, and shot with a bow and arrows. And he was a very good shot too.

Besides this he collected stamps and birds' eggs and picture post-cards, and kept guinea-pigs and bantams, and climbed trees and tore his clothes in twenty different ways. And once he fought the grocer's boy and got licked and didn't cry, and made friends with the grocer's boy afterwards, and got him to show him all he knew about fighting, so you see he was really not a mug. He was ten years old and he had enjoyed every moment of his ten years, even the sleeping ones, because he always dreamed jolly dreams, though he could not always remember what they were.

I tell you all this so that you may understand why he said what he did when his mother broke the news to him.

He was sitting by the stream that ran along the end of the garden, making bricks of the clay that the stream's banks were made of. He dried them in the sun, and then baked them under the kitchen stove. (It is quite a good way to make bricks – you might try it sometimes.) His mother came out, looking just as usual, in her pink cotton gown and her pink sunbonnet; and she had a letter in her hand.

'Hullo, boy of my heart,' she said, 'very busy?'

'Yes,' said Quentin importantly, not looking up, and going on with his work. 'I'm making stones to build Stonehenge with. You'll show me how to build it, won't you, mother.'

'Yes, dear,' she said absently. 'Yes, if I can.'

'Of course you can,' he said, 'you can do everything.'

She sat down on a tuft of grass near him.

'Quentin dear,' she said, and something in her voice made him look up suddenly.

'Oh, mother, what is it?' he asked.

'Daddy's been wounded,' she said; 'he's all right now, dear – don't be frightened. Only I've got to go out to him. I shall meet him in Egypt. And you must go to school in Salisbury, a very nice school, dear, till I come back.'

'Can't I come too?' he asked.

And when he understood that he could not he went on with the bricks in silence, with his mouth shut very tight.

After a moment he said, 'Salisbury? Then I shall see Stonehenge?'

'Yes,' said his mother, pleased that he took the news so calmly, 'you will be sure to see Stone-henge some time.'

He stood still, looking down at the little mould of clay in his hand – so still that his mother got up and came close to him.

'Quentin,' she said, 'darling, what is it?'

He leaned his head against her.

'I won't make a fuss,' he said, 'but you can't

begin to be brave the very first minute. Or, if you do, you can't go on being.'

And with that he began to cry, though he had not cried after the affair of the grocer's boy.

The thought of school was not so terrible to Quentin as Mrs de Ward had thought it would be. In fact, he rather liked it, with half his mind; but the other half didn't like it, because it meant parting from his mother who, so far, had been his only friend. But it was exciting to be taken to Southampton, and have all sorts of new clothes bought for you, and a school trunk, and a little polished box that locked up, to keep your money in and your gold sleeve links, and your watch and chain when you were not wearing them.

Also the journey to Salisbury was made in a motor, which was very exciting of course, and rather took Quentin's mind off the parting with his mother, as she meant it should. And there was a very grand lunch at The White Hart Hotel at Salisbury, and then, very suddenly indeed, it was goodbye, goodbye, and the motor snorted, and hooted, and throbbed, and rushed away, and mother was gone, and Quentin was at school.

I believe it was quite a nice school. It was in a very nice house with a large quiet garden, and there were only about twenty boys. And the masters were kind, and the boys no worse than other boys of their age. But Quentin hated it from the very beginning. For when his mother had gone the Headmaster said: 'School will be out in half-an-hour; take a book, de Ward,' and gave him *Little Eric and his Friends*, a mere baby book. It was too silly. He could not read it. He saw on a shelf near him, *Smith's Antiquities*, a very old friend of his, so he said: 'I'd rather have this, please.'

'You should say "sir" when you speak to a master,' the Head said to him. 'Take the book by all means.' To himself the Head said, 'I wish you joy of it, you little prig.'

When school was over, one of the boys was told to show Quentin his bed and his locker. The matron had already unpacked his box and his pile of books was waiting for him to carry it over.

'Golly, what a lot of books,' said Smithson minor. 'What's this? *Atlantis*? Is it a jolly story?'

'It isn't a story,' said Quentin. And just then the classical master came by. 'What's that about *Atlantis*?' he said.

'It's a book the new chap's got,' said Smithson.

The classical master glanced at the book.

'And how much do you understand of this?' he asked, fluttering the leaves.

'Nearly all, I think,' said Quentin.

'You should say "sir" when you speak to a master,' said the classical one; and to himself he added, 'little prig.' Then he said to Quentin: 'I am afraid you will find yourself rather out of your element among ordinary boys.'

'I don't think so,' said Quentin calmly, adding as an afterthought, 'sir'.

'I'm glad you're so confident,' said the classical master and went.

'My word,' said Smithson minor in a rather awed voice, 'you did answer him back.'

'Of course I did,' said Quentin. 'Don't *you* answer when you're spoken to?'

Smithson minor informed the interested school that the new chap was a prig, but he had a cool cheek, and that some sport might be expected.

After supper the boys had half an hour's recreation. Quentin, who was tired, picked up a book which a big boy had just put down. It was the *Midsummer Night's Dream*.

'Hi, you kid,' said the big boy, 'don't pretend you read Shakespeare for fun. That's simple swank, you know.'

'I don't know what swank is,' said Quentin, 'but I like the *Midsummer* whoever wrote it.'

'Whoever *what*?'

'Well,' said Quentin, 'there's a good deal to be said for its being Bacon who wrote the plays.'

Of course that settled it. From that moment, he was called not de Ward, which was strange enough, but Bacon. He rather liked that. But the next day it was Pork, and the day after Pig, and that was unbearable.

He was at the bottom of his class, for he knew no Latin as it is taught in schools, only odd words that English words come from, and some Latin words that are used in science. And I cannot pretend that his arithmetic was anything but contemptible.

The book called *Atlantis* had been looked at by most of the school, and Smithson major, not nearly such an agreeable boy as his brother, hit on a new nickname.

'Atlantic Pork's a good name for a swanker,' he said. 'You know the rotten meat they have in Chicago.'

This was in the playground before dinner. Quentin, who had to keep his mouth shut very tight these days, because, of course, a boy of ten cannot cry before other chaps, shut the book he was reading and looked up.

'I won't be called that,' he said quietly.

'Who said you wouldn't?' said Smithson major, who, after all, was only twelve. 'I say you will.'

'If you call me that I shall hit you,' said Quentin, 'as hard as I can.'

A roar of laughter went up, and cries of, 'Poor old Smithson' – 'Apologize, Smithie, and leave the omnibus.'

'And what should I being doing while you were hitting me?' asked Smithson contemptuously.

'I don't know and I don't care,' said Quentin.

Smithson looked round. No master was in sight. It seemed an excellent opportunity to teach young de Ward his place.

'Atlantic pig-swine,' he said very deliberately.

And Quentin sprang at him, and instantly it was a fight.

Now Quentin had only once fought – really fought – before. Then it was the grocer's boy and he had been beaten. But he had learned something since. And the chief conclusion he now drew from his memories of that fight was that he had not hit half hard enough, an opinion almost universal among those who have fought and not won.

As the fist of Smithson major described a half circle and hurt his ear very much, Quentin suddenly screwed himself up and hit out with his right hand, straight, and with his whole weight behind the blow as the grocer's boy had shown him. All his grief for his wounded father, his sorrow at the parting from his mother, and all his hatred of his school, and his contempt for his schoolfellows went into that blow. It landed on the point of the chin of Smithson major who fell together like a heap of rags.

'Oh,' said Quentin, gazing with interest at his hand – it hurt a good deal but he looked at it with respect – 'I'm afraid I've hurt him.'

He had forgotten for a moment that he was in an enemies' country, and so, apparently, had his enemies.

'Well done, Piggy! Bravo, young 'un! Well hit, by Jove!'

Friendly hands thumped him on the back. Smithson major was no popular hero.

Quentin felt – as his schoolfellows would have

put it – bucked. It is one thing to be called Pig in enmity and derision. Another to be called Piggy – an affectionate diminutive, after all – to the chorus of admiring smacks.

'Get up, Smithie,' cried the ring. 'Want any more?'

It appeared that Smithie did not want any more. He lay, not moving at all, and very white.

'I say,' the crowd's temper veered, 'you've killed him, I expect. I wouldn't like to be you, Bacon.'

Pig, you notice, for aggravation – Piggy in enthusiastic applause. In the moment of possible tragedy the more formal Bacon.

'I haven't,' said Quentin, very white himself, 'but if I have he began – by calling names.'

Smithson moved and grunted. A sigh of relief swept the ring as a breeze sweeps a cornfield.

'He's all right. A fair knock-out. Piggy's got the use of 'em. Do Smithie good.' The voices hushed suddenly. A master was on the scene – the classical master.

'Fighting?' he said. 'The new boy? Who began it?'

'I did,' said Quentin, 'but he began with calling names.'

'Sneak!' murmured the entire school, and Quentin, who had seen no reason for not speaking the truth, perceived that one should not tell all one knows, and that once more he stood alone in the world.

'You will go to your room, de Ward,' said the

classical master, bending over Smithson, who having been 'knocked silly' still remained in that condition, 'and the headmaster will consider your case tomorrow. You will probably be expelled.'

Quentin went to his room and thought over his position. It seemed to be desperate. How was he to know that the classical master was even then saying to the Head:

'He's got something in him, prig or not prig, sir.'

'You were quite right to send him to his room,' said the Head, 'discipline must be maintained, as Mr Ducket says. But it will do Smithson major a world of good. A boy who reads Shakespeare for fun, and has views about Atlantis, and can knock out a bully as well . . . He'll be a power in the school. But we mustn't let him know it.'

That was rather a pity. Because Quentin, furious at the injustice of the whole thing – Smithson, the aggressor, consoled with; himself punished; expulsion threatened – was maturing plans.

'If mother had known what it was like,' he said to himself, 'she would never have left me here. I've got the two pounds she gave me. I shall go to the White Hart at Salisbury . . . no, they'd find me then. I'll go to Lyndhurst and write to her. It's better to run away than to be expelled. Quentin Durward would never have waited to be expelled from anywhere.'

Of course Quentin Durward was my hero's

hero. It could not be otherwise since his own name was so like that of the Scottish guardsman.

Now the school in Salisbury was a little school for little boys – boys who were used to schools and took the rough with the smooth. But Quentin was not used to schools, and he had taken the rough very much to heart. So much that he did not mean to take any more of it.

His dinner was brought up on a tray – bread and water. He put the bread in his pocket. Then when he knew that everyone was at dinner in the long dining-room at the back of the house, he just walked very quietly down the stairs, opened the side door and marched out, down the garden path and out at the tradesmen's gate. He knew better than to shut either gate or door.

He went quickly down the street, turned the first corner he came to so as to get out of sight of the school. He turned another corner, went through an archway, and found himself in an inn-yard – very quiet indeed. Only a liver-coloured lurcher dog wagged a sleepy tail on the hot flag-stones.

Quentin was just turning to go back through the arch, for there was no other way out of the yard, when he saw a big covered cart, whose horse wore a nose-bag and looked as if there was no hurry. The cart bore the name, 'Miles, Carrier, Lyndhurst'.

Quentin knew all about lifts. He had often begged them and got them. Now there was no one to ask. But he felt he could very well explain later that he had wanted a lift, much better than now, in fact, when he might be caught at any moment by someone from the school.

He climbed up by the shaft. There were boxes and packages of all sorts in the cart, and at the back an empty crate with sacking over it. He got into the crate, pulled the sacking over himself, and settled down to eat his bread.

Presently the carrier came out, and there was talk, slow, long-drawn talk. After a long while the cart shook to the carrier's heavy climb into it, the harness rattled, the cart lurched, and the wheels were loud and bumpy over the cobble stones of the yard.

Quentin felt safe. The glow of anger was still hot in him, and he was glad to think how they would look for him all over the town, in vain. He lifted the sacking at one corner so that he could look out between the canvas of the cart's back and side, and hoped to see the classical master distractedly looking for him. But the streets were very sleepy. Everyone in Salisbury was having dinner – or in the case of the affluent, lunch.

The black horse seemed as sleepy as the streets, and went very slowly. Also it stopped very often, and wherever there were parcels to leave there was slow, long talkings to be exchanged. I think, perhaps, Quentin dozed a good deal under his sacks. At any rate it was with a shock of surprise that he suddenly heard the carrier's voice saying, as the horse stopped with a jerk:

'There's a crate for you, Mrs Baddock, returned empty,' and knew that that crate was not empty, but full – full of boy.

'I'll go and call Joe,' said a voice – Mrs Baddock's, Quentin supposed, and slow feet stumped away over stones. Mr Miles leisurely untied the tail of the cart, ready to let the crate be taken out.

Quentin spent a paralytic moment. What could he do?

And then, luckily or unluckily, a reckless motor tore past, and the black horse plunged and Mr Miles had to go to its head and 'talk pretty' to it for a minute. And in that minute Quentin lifted the sacking, and looked out. It was low sunset, and the street was deserted. He stepped out of the crate, dropped to the ground, and slipped behind a stout and friendly water-butt that seemed to offer protective shelter.

Joe came, and the crate was taken down.

'You haven't seen nothing of that there runaway boy by chance?' said a new voice – Joe's no doubt.

'What boy?' said Mr Miles.

'Run away from school, Salisbury,' said Joe. 'Telegrams far and near, so they be. Little varmint.'

'I ain't seen no boys, not more'n ordinary,' said Mr Miles. 'Thick as flies they be, here, there, and everywhere, drat 'em. Sixpence – Correct. So long, Joe.'

The cart rattled away. Joe and the crate blundered out of hearing, and Quentin looked cautiously round the water-butt.

This was an adventure. But he was cooler now than he had been at starting – his hot anger had died down. He would have been contented, he could not help feeling, with a less adventurous adventure.

But he was in for it now. He felt, as I suppose people feel when they jump off cliffs with parachutes, that return was impossible.

Hastily turning his school cap inside out – the only disguise he could think of, he emerged from the water-butt seclusion and into the street, trying to look as if there was no reason why he should not be there. He did not know the village. It was not Lyndhurst. And of course asking the way was not to be thought of.

There was a piece of sacking lying on the road; it must have dropped from the carrier's cart. He picked it up and put it over his shoulders.

'A deeper disguise,' he said, and walked on.

He walked steadily for a long, long way as it seemed, and the world got darker and darker. But he kept on. Surely he must presently come to some village, or some signpost.

Anyhow, whatever happened, he could not go back. That was the one certain thing. The broad stretches of country to right and left held no shapes of houses, no glimmer of warm candle-light; they were bare and bleak, only broken by circles of trees that stood out like black islands in the misty grey of the twilight.

'I shall have to sleep behind a hedge,' he said bravely enough; but there did not seem to be any hedges. And then, quite suddenly, he came upon it.

A scattered building, half transparent as it seemed, showing black against the last faint pink and primrose of the sunset. He stopped, took a few steps off the road on short, crisp turf that rose in a gentle slope. And at the end of a dozen paces he knew it. Stonehenge! Stonehenge he had always wanted so desperately to see. Well, he saw it now, more or less.

He stopped to think. He knew that Stonehenge stands all alone on Salisbury Plain. He was very tired. His mother had told him about a girl in a book who slept all night on the altar stone at Stonehenge. So it was a thing that people did – to sleep there. He was not afraid, as you or I might have been – of that lonely desolate ruin of a temple of long ago. He was used to the forest, and, compared with the forest, any building is homelike.

There was just enough light left amid the stones of the wonderful broken circle to guide him to its centre. As he went his hand brushed a plant; he caught at it, and a little group of flowers came away in his hand.

'St John's wort,' he said, 'that's the magic

flower.' And he remembered that it is only magic when you pluck it on Midsummer Eve.

'And this *is* Midsummer Eve,' he told himself, and put it in his buttonhole.

'I don't know where the altar stone is,' he said, 'but that looks a cosy little crack between those two big stones.'

He crept into it, and lay down on a flat stone that stretched between and under two fallen pillars.

The night was soft and warm; it was Midsummer Eve.

'Mother isn't going till the twenty-sixth,' he told himself. 'I shan't bother about hotels. I shall send her a telegram in the morning, and get a carriage at the nearest stables and go straight back to her. No, she won't be angry when she hears all about it. I'll ask her to let me go to sea instead of to school. It's much more manly. Much more manly . . . much much more, much.'

He was asleep. And the wild west wind that swept across the plain spared the little corner where he lay asleep, curled up in his sacking with the inside-out school cap, doubled twice, for pillow.

He fell asleep on the smooth, solid, steady stone.

He awoke on the stone in a world that rocked as sea-boats rock on a choppy sea.

He went to sleep between fallen moveless pillars of a ruin older than any world that history knows.

He awoke in the shade of a purple awning through which strong sunlight filtered, and purple curtains that flapped and strained in the wind; and there was a smell, a sweet familiar smell, of tarred ropes and the sea.

'I say,' said Quentin to himself, 'here's a rum go.'

He had learned that expression in a school in Salisbury, a long time ago as it seemed.

The stone on which he lay dipped and rose to a rhythm which he knew well enough. He had felt it when he and his mother went in a little boat from Keyhaven to Alum Bay in the Isle of Wight. There was no doubt in his mind. He was on a ship. But how, but why? Who could have carried him all that way without waking him? Was it magic? Accidental magic? The St John's wort perhaps? And the stone – it was not the same. It was new, clean cut, and, where the wind displaced a corner of the curtain, dazzlingly white in the sunlight.

There was the pat pat of bare feet on the deck, a dull sort of shuffling as though people were arranging themselves. And then people outside the awning began to sing. It was a strange song, not at all like any music you or I have ever heard. It had no tune, no more tune than a drum has, or a trumpet, but it had a sort of wild rough glorious exciting splendour about it, and gave you the sort of intense all-alive feeling that drums and trumpets give.

Quentin lifted a corner of the purple curtain and looked out.

Instantly the song stopped, drowned in the deepest silence Quentin had ever imagined. It was only broken by the flip-flapping of the sheets against the masts of the ship. For it was a ship, Quentin saw that as the bulwark dipped to show him an unending waste of sea, broken by bigger waves than he had ever dreamed of. He saw also a crowd of men, dressed in white and blue and purple and gold. Their right arms were raised towards the sun, half of whose face showed across the sea – but they seemed to be, as my old nurse used to say, 'struck so', for their eyes were not fixed on the sun, but on Quentin. And not in anger, he noticed curiously, but with surprise and . . . could it be that they were afraid of him?

Quentin was shivering with the surprise and newness of it all. He had read about magic, but he had not wholly believed in it, and yet, now, if this was not magic, what was it? You go to sleep on an old stone in a ruin. You wake on the same stone, quite new, on a ship. Magic, magic, if ever there was magic in this wonderful, mysterious world!

The silence became awkward. Someone had to say something.

'Good-morning,' said Quentin, feeling that he ought perhaps to be the one.

Instantly everyone in sight fell on his face on the deck.

Only one, a tall man with a black beard and a

blue mantle, stood up and looked Quentin in the eyes.

'Who are you?' he said. 'Answer, I adjure you by the Sacred Tau!' Now this was very odd, and Quentin could never understand it, but when this man spoke Quentin understood *him* perfectly, and yet at the same time he knew that the man was speaking a foreign language. So that his thought was not, 'Hullo, you speak English!' but 'Hullo, I can understand your language.'

'I am Quentin de Ward,' he said.

'A name from other stars! How came you here?' asked the blue-mantled man.

'*I* don't know,' said Quentin.

'He does not know. He did not sail with us. It is by magic that he is here,' said Blue Mantle. 'Rise, all, and greet the Chosen of the Gods.'

They rose from the deck, and Quentin saw that they were all bearded men, with bright, earnest eyes, dressed in strange dress of something like jersey and tunic and heavy golden ornaments.

'Hail! Chosen of the Gods,' cried Blue Mantle, who seemed to be the leader.

'Hail, Chosen of the Gods!' echoed the rest.

'Thank you very much, I'm sure,' said Quentin.

'And what is this stone?' asked Blue Mantle, pointing to the stone on which Quentin sat.

And Quentin, anxious to show off his knowledge, said:

'I'm not quite sure, but I *think* it's the altar stone of Stonehenge.'

'It is proved,' said Blue Mantle. 'Thou art the Chosen of the Gods. Is there anything my Lord needs?' he added humbly.

'I . . . I'm rather hungry,' said Quentin; 'it's a long time since dinner, you know.'

They brought him bread and bananas, and oranges.

'Take,' said Blue Mantle, 'of the fruits of the earth, and specially of this, which gives drink and meat and ointment to man,' suddenly offering a large cocoa-nut.

Quentin took, with appropriate 'Thank you's' and 'You're very kind's'.

'Nothing,' said Blue Mantle, 'is too good for the Chosen of the Gods. All that we have is yours, to the very last day of your life you have only to command, and we obey. You will like to eat in seclusion. And afterwards you will let us behold the whole person of the Chosen of the Gods.'

Quentin retired into the purple tent, with the fruits and the cocoa-nut. As you know, a cocoa-nut is not handy to get at the inside of, at the best of times, so Quentin set that aside, meaning to ask Blue Mantle later on for a gimlet and a hammer.

When he had had enough to eat he peeped out again. Blue Mantle was on the watch and came quickly forward.

'Now,' said he, very crossly indeed, 'tell me how you got here. This Chosen of the Gods business is all very well for the vulgar. But you and I know that there is no such thing as magic.'

'Speak for yourself,' said Quentin. 'If I'm not here by magic I'm not here at all.'

'Yes, you are,' said Blue Mantle.

'I know I am,' said Quentin, 'but if I'm not here by magic what am I here by?'

'Stowawayishness,' said Blue Mantle.

'If you think that why don't you treat me as a stowaway?'

'Because of public opinion,' said Blue Mantle, rubbing his nose in an angry sort of perplexedness.

'Very well,' said Quentin, who was feeling so surprised and bewildered that it was a real relief to him to bully somebody. 'Now look here. I came here by magic, accidental magic. I belong to quite a different world from yours. But perhaps you are right about my being the Chosen of the Gods. And I shan't tell you anything about my world. But I command you, by the Sacred Tau' (he had been quick enough to catch and remember the word), 'to tell me who you are, and where you come from, and where you are going.'

Blue Mantle shrugged his shoulders. 'Oh, well,' he said, 'if you invoke the sacred names of Power . . . But I don't call it fair play. Especially as you know perfectly well, and just want to browbeat me into telling lies. I shall not tell lies. I shall tell you the truth.'

'I hoped you would,' said Quentin gently.

'Well then,' said Blue Mantle, 'I am a Priest of Poseidon, and I come from the great and immortal kingdom of Atlantis.'

'From the temple where the gold statue is, with the twelve sea-horses in gold?' Quentin asked eagerly.

'Ah, I knew you knew all about it,' said Blue Mantle, 'so I don't need to tell you that I am taking the sacred stone, on which you are sitting (profanely if you are a mere stowaway, and not the Chosen of the Gods) to complete the splendid structure of a temple built on a great plain in the second of the islands which are our colonies in the North East.'

'Tell me all about Atlantis,' said Quentin. And the priest, protesting that Quentin knew as much about it as he did, told.

And all the time the ship was ploughing through the waves, sometimes sailing, sometimes rowed by hidden rowers with long oars. And Quentin was served in all things as though he had been a king. If he had insisted that he was not the Chosen of the Gods everything might have been different. But he did not. And he was very anxious to show how much he knew about Atlantis. And sometimes he was wrong, the Priest said, but much more often he was right.

'We are less than three days' journey now from the Eastern Isles,' Blue Mantle said one day, 'and I warn you that if you are a mere stowaway you had better own it. Because if you persist in calling yourself the Chosen of the Gods you will be expected to act as such – to the very end.'

'I don't call myself anything,' said Quentin, 'though I am not a stowaway, anyhow, and I don't know how I came here – so of course it was magic. It's simply silly your being so cross. *I* can't help being here. Let's be friends.'

'Well,' said Blue Mantle, much less crossly, 'I never believed in magic, though I *am* a priest, but if it is, it is. We may as well be friends, as you call it. It isn't for very long, anyway,' he added mysteriously.

And then to show his friendliness he took Quentin all over the ship, and explained it all to him. And Quentin enjoyed himself thoroughly, though every now and then he had to pinch himself to make sure that he was awake. And he was fed well all the time, and all the time made much of, so that when the ship reached land he was quite sorry. The ship anchored by a stone quay, most solid and serviceable, and everyone was very busy.

Quentin kept out of sight behind the purple curtains. The sailors and the priests and the priests' attendants and everybody on the boat had asked him so many questions, and been so curious about his clothes, that he was not anxious to hear any more questions asked, or to have to invent answers to them.

And after a very great deal of talk – almost as much as Mr Miles's carrying had needed – the altar stone was lifted, Quentin, curtains, awning and all, and carried along a gangway to the shore, and there it was put on a sort of cart, more like what people in Manchester call a lurry than anything else I can think of. The wheels were made of solid circles of wood bound round with copper. And the cart was drawn by – not horses or donkeys or oxen or even dogs – but by an enormous creature more like an elephant than anything else, only it had long hair rather like the hair worn by goats.

You, perhaps, would not have known what this vast creature was, but Quentin, who had all sorts of out-of-the-way information packed in his head, knew at once that it was a mammoth.

And by that he knew, too, that he had slipped back many thousands of years, because, of course, it is a very long time indeed since there were any mammoths alive, and able to draw lurries. And the cart and the priest and the priest's retinue and the stone and Quentin and the mammoth journeyed slowly away from the coast, passing through great green forests and among strange grey mountains.

Where were they journeying?

Quentin asked the same question you may be sure, and Blue Mantle told him:

'To Stonehenge.' And Quentin understood him perfectly, though Stonehenge was not the word Blue Mantle used, or anything like it.

'The great temple is now complete,' he said, 'all but the altar stone. It will be the most wonderful temple ever built in any of the Colonies of Atlantis. And it will be consecrated on the longest day of the year.'

'Midsummer Day,' said Quentin thoughtlessly – and, as usual, anxious to tell all he knew. 'I know. The sun strikes through the arch on to the altar stone at sunrise. Hundreds of people go to see it: the ruins are quite crowded sometimes, I believe.'

'Ruins?' said the priest in a terrible voice. 'Crowded? Ruins?'

'I mean,' said Quentin hastily, 'the sun will still shine the same way even when the temple is in ruins, won't it?'

'The temple', said the priest, 'is built to defy time. It will never be in ruins.'

'That's all *you* know,' said Quentin, not very politely.

'It is not by any means all I know,' said the priest. 'I do not tell all I know. Nor do you.'

'I used to,' said Quentin, 'but I shan't any more. It only leads to trouble – I see that now.'

Now, though Quentin had been intensely interested in everything he had seen in the ship and on the journey, you may be sure he had not lost sight of the need there was to get back out of this time of Atlantis into his own time. He knew that he must have got into these Atlantean times by some very simple accidental magic, and he felt no doubt that he should get back in the same way. He felt almost sure that the reverse-action, so to speak, of the magic would begin when the stone got back to the place where it had lain for so many thousand years before he happened to go to sleep on it, and to start – perhaps by the St John's wort – the accidental magic. If only, when he got back there he could think of the compelling, the magic word!

And now the slow procession wound over the downs, and far away across the plain, which was almost just the same then as it is now, Quentin saw what he knew must be Stonehenge. But it was no longer the grey pile of ruins that you have perhaps seen – or have, at any rate, seen pictures of.

From afar one could see the gleam of yellow gold and red copper; the flutter of purple curtains, the glitter and dazzle of shimmering silver.

As they drew near to the spot Quentin perceived that the great stones he remembered were overlaid with ornamental work, with vivid, bright-coloured paintings. The whole thing was a great circular building, every stone in its place. At a mile or two distant lay a town. And in that town, with every possible luxury, served with every circumstance of servile homage, Quentin ate and slept.

I wish I had time to tell you what that town was like where he slept and ate, but I have not. You can read for yourself, some day, what Atlantis was like. Plato tells us a good deal, and the Colonies of Atlantis must have had at least a reasonable second-rate copy of the cities of that fair and lovely land.

That night, for the first time since he had first gone to sleep on the altar stone, Quentin slept apart from it. He lay on a wooden couch strewn with soft bear-skins, and a woollen coverlet was laid over him. And he slept soundly.

In the middle of the night, as it seemed, Blue Mantle woke him.

'Come,' he said, 'Chosen of the Gods – since you *will* be that, and no stowaway – the hour draws nigh.'

The mammoth was waiting. Quentin and Blue Mantle rode on its back to the outer porch of the new temple of Stonehenge. Rows of priests and attendants, robed in white and blue and purple, formed a sort of avenue up which Blue Mantle led the Chosen of the Gods, who was Quentin. They took off his jacket and put a white dress on him, rather like a night-shirt without sleeves. And they put a thick wreath of London Pride on his head and another, larger and longer, round his neck.

'If only the chaps at school could see me now!' he said to himself proudly.

And by this time it was grey dawn.

'Lie down now,' said Blue Mantle, 'lie down, O Beloved of the Gods, upon the altar stone, for the last time.'

'I shall be able to go, then?' Quentin asked. This accidental magic was, he perceived, a tricky thing, and he wanted to be sure.

'You will not be able to stay,' said the priest. 'If

going is what you desire, the desire of the Chosen of the Gods is fully granted.'

The grass on the plain far and near rustled with the tread of many feet; the cold air of dawn thrilled to the awed murmur of many voices.

Quentin lay down, with his pink wreaths and his white robe, and watched the quickening pinkiness of the East. And slowly the great circle of the temple filled with white-robed folk, all carrying in their hands the faint pinkiness of the flowers which we nowadays call London Pride.

And all eyes were fixed on the arch through which, at sunrise on Midsummer Day, the sun's first beam should fall upon the white, new, clean altar stone. The stone is still there, after all these thousands of years, and at sunrise on Midsummer Day the sun's first ray still falls on it.

The sky grew lighter and lighter, and at last the sun peered redly over the down, and the first ray of the morning sunlight fell full on the altar stone and on the face of Quentin.

And, as it did so, a very tall, white-robed priest with a deer-skin apron and a curious winged head-dress stepped forward. He carried a great bronze knife, and he waved it ten times in the shaft of sunlight that shot through the arch and on to the altar stone.

'Thus,' he cried, 'thus do I bathe the sacred blade in the pure fountain of all light, all wisdom, all splendour. In the name of the ten kings, the ten virtues, the ten hopes, the ten fears I make my weapon clean! May this temple of our love and our desire endure for ever, so long as the glory of our Lord the Sun is shed upon this earth. May the sacrifice I now humbly and proudly offer be acceptable to the gods by whom it has been so miraculously provided. Chosen of the Gods! return to the gods who sent thee!'

A roar of voices rang through the temple. The bronze knife was raised over Quentin. He could not believe that this, this, this horror, was the end of all these wonderful happenings.

'No – no,' he cried, 'it's not true. I'm not the Chosen of the Gods! I'm only a little boy that's got here by accidental magic!'

'Silence,' cried the priest, 'Chosen of the Immortals, close your eyes! It will not hurt. This life is only a dream; the other life is the real life. Be strong, be brave!'

Quentin was not brave. But he shut his eyes. He could not help it. The glitter of the bronze knife in the sunlight was too strong for him.

He could not believe that this could really have happened to him. Everyone had been so kind – so friendly to him. And it was all for this!

Suddenly a sharp touch at his side told him that for this, indeed, it had all been. He felt the point of the knife.

'Mother!' he cried. And opened his eyes again.

He always felt quite sure afterwards that 'Mother' was the master-word, the spell of spells. For when he opened his eyes there was no priest, no white-robed worshippers, no splendour of colour and metal, no Chosen of the Gods, no knife – only a little boy with a piece of sacking over him, damp with the night dews, lying on a stone amid the grey ruins of Stonehenge, and, all about him, a crowd of tourists who had come to see the sun's first shaft strike the age-old altar of Stonehenge on Midsummer Day in the morning. And instead of a knife-point at his side there was only the ferrule of the umbrella of an elderly and retired tea merchant in a mackintosh and an Alpine hat – a ferrule which had prodded the sleeping boy so unexpectedly surprised on the very altar stone where the sun's ray now lingered.

And then, in a moment, he knew that he had not uttered the spell in vain, the word of compelling, the word of power: for his mother was there kneeling beside him. I am sorry to say that he cried as he clung to her. *We* cannot all of us be brave, always.

The tourists were very kind and interested, and the tea merchant insisted on giving Quentin something out of a flask, which was so nasty that Quentin only pretended to drink, out of politeness. His mother had a carriage waiting, and they escaped to it while the tourists were saying, 'How romantic!' and asking each other whatever in the world had happened.

'But how *did* you come to be there, darling?' said his mother with warm hands comfortingly round him. 'I've been looking for you all night. I went to say goodbye to you yesterday – Oh, Quentin – and I found you'd run away. How *could* you?'

'I'm sorry', said Quentin, 'if it worried you, I'm sorry. Very, very. I was going to telegraph today.'

'But where have you been? What have you been doing all night?' she asked, caressing him.

'Is it only one night?' said Quentin. 'I don't know exactly what's happened. It was accidental magic, I think, mother. I'm glad I thought of the right word to get back, though.' And then he told her all about it. She held him very tightly and let him talk.

Perhaps she thought that a little boy to whom accidental magic happened all in a minute, like that, was not exactly the right little boy for that excellent school in Salisbury. Anyhow she took him to Egypt with her to meet his father, and, on the way, they happened to see a doctor in London who said: 'Nerves' which is a poor name for accidental magic, and Quentin does not believe it means the same thing at all.

Quentin's father is well now, and he has left the army, and father and mother and Quentin live in a jolly, little, old house in Salisbury, and Quentin is a 'day boy' at that very same school. He and Smithson minor are the greatest of friends. But he has never told Smithson minor about the accidental magic. He has learned now, and learned very thoroughly, that it is not always wise to tell all you know. If he had not owned that he knew that it was the Stonehenge altar stone!

You may think that the accidental magic was all a dream, and that Quentin dreamed it because his mother had told him so much about Atlantis. But then, how do you account for his dreaming so much that his mother had never told him? You think that that part wasn't true, well, it may have been true for anything I know. And I am sure you don't know more about it than I do.

4

THE PRINCESS AND THE HEDGE-PIG

'But I don't see what we're to *do*,' said the Queen for the twentieth time.

'Whatever we do will end in misfortune,' said the King gloomily; 'you'll see it will.'

They were sitting in the honeysuckle arbour talking things over, while the nurse walked up and down the terrace with the new baby in her arms.

'Yes, dear,' said the poor Queen; 'I've not the slightest doubt I shall.'

Misfortune comes in many ways, and you can't always know beforehand that a certain way is the way misfortune will come by: but there are things misfortune comes after as surely as night comes after day. For instance, if you let all the water boil away, the kettle will have a hole burnt in it. If you leave the bath taps running and the waste-pipe closed, the stairs of your house will, sooner or later, resemble Niagara. If you leave your purse at home, you won't have it with you when you want to pay your tram-fare. And if you throw lighted wax matches at your muslin curtains, your parent will most likely have to pay five pounds to the fire engines for coming round and blowing the fire out with a wet hose. Also if you are a king and do not invite the wicked fairy to your christening parties, she will come all the same. And if you do ask the wicked fairy, she will come, and in either case it will be the worse for the new princess. So what is a poor monarch to do? Of course there is one way out of the difficulty, and that is not to have a christening party at all. But this offends all the good fairies, and then where are you?

All these reflections had presented themselves to the minds of King Ozymandias and his Queen, and neither of them could deny that they were in a most awkward situation. They were 'talking it over' for the hundredth time on the palace terrace where the pomegranates and oleanders grew in green tubs and the marble balustrade is overgrown with roses, red and white and pink and yellow. On the lower terrace the royal nurse was walking up and down with the baby princess that all the fuss was about. The Queen's eyes followed the baby admiringly.

'The darling!' she said. 'Oh, Ozymandias, don't you sometimes wish we'd been poor people?'

'Never!' said the King decidedly.

'Well, I do,' said the Queen; 'then we could have had just you and me and your sister at the christening, and no fear of – oh! I've thought of something.'

The King's patient expression showed that he did not think it likely that she would have thought of anything useful; but at the first five words his expression changed. You would have said that he pricked up his ears, if kings had ears that could be pricked up. What she said was:

'Let's have a secret christening.'

'How?' asked the King.

The Queen was gazing in the direction of the baby with what is called a 'far away look' in her eyes.

'Wait a minute,' she said slowly. 'I see it all – yes – we'll have the party in the cellars – you know they're splendid.'

'My great-grandfather had them built by Lancashire men, yes,' interrupted the King.

'We'll send out the invitations to look like bills. The baker's boy can take them. He's a very nice boy. He made baby laugh yesterday when I was explaining to him about the Standard Bread. We'll just put "1 loaf 3. A remittance at your earliest convenience will oblige." That'll mean that 1 person is invited for 3 o'clock, and on the back we'll write where and why in invisible ink. Lemon juice, you know. And the baker's boy shall be told to ask to see the people – just as they do when they *really* mean earliest convenience – and then he shall just whisper: "Deadly secret. Lemon juice. Hold it to the fire," and come away. Oh, dearest, do say you approve!'

The King laid down his pipe, set his crown straight, and kissed the Queen with great and serious earnestness.

'You are a wonder,' he said. 'It is the very thing. But the baker's boy is very small. Can we trust him?'

'He is nine,' said the Queen, 'and I have sometimes thought that he must be a prince in disguise. He is so very intelligent.'

The Queen's plan was carried out. The cellars, which were really extraordinarily fine, were secretly decorated by the King's confidential man and the Queen's confidential maid and a few of *their* confidential friends whom they knew they could really trust. You would never have thought they were cellars when the decorations were finished. The walls were hung with white satin and white velvet, with wreaths of white roses, and the stone floors were covered with freshly cut turf with white daisies, brisk and neat, growing in it.

The invitations were duly delivered by the baker's boy. On them was written in plain blue ink.

'THE ROYAL BAKERIES
'1 loaf 3d.
'An early remittance will oblige.'

And when the people held the letter to the fire, as they were whisperingly instructed to do by the baker's boy, they read in a faint brown writing:

'King Ozymandias and Queen Eliza invite you to the christening of their daughter Princess

Ozyliza at three on Wednesday in the Palace cellars.

'*PS* – We are obliged to be very secret and careful because of wicked fairies, so please come disguised as a tradesman with a bill, calling for the last time before it leaves your hands.'

You will understand by this that the King and Queen were not as well off as they could wish; so that tradesmen calling at the palace with that sort of message was the last thing likely to excite remark. But as most of the King's subjects were not very well off either, this was merely a bond between the King and his people. They could sympathize with each other, and understand each other's troubles in a way impossible to most kings and most nations.

You can imagine the excitement in the families of the people who were invited to the christening party, and the interest they felt in their costumes. The Lord Chief Justice disguised himself as a shoemaker; he still had his old blue brief-bag by him, and a brief-bag and a boot-bag are very much alike. The Commander-in-Chief dressed as a dog's meat man and wheeled a barrow. The Prime Minister appeared as a tailor; this required no change of dress and only a slight change of expression. And the other courtiers all disguised themselves perfectly. So did the good fairies, who had, of course, been invited first of all. Benevola, Queen of the Good Fairies, disguised herself as a moonbeam, which can go into any palace and no questions asked. Serena, the next in command, dressed as a butterfly, and all the other fairies had disguises equally pretty and tasteful.

The Queen looked most kind and beautiful, the King very handsome and manly, and all the guests agreed that the new princess was the most beautiful baby they had ever seen in all their born days.

Everybody brought the most charming christening presents concealed beneath their disguises. The fairies gave the usual gifts, beauty, grace, intelligence, charm, and so on.

Everything seemed to be going better than well. But of course you know it wasn't. The Lord High Admiral had not been able to get a cook's dress large enough completely to cover his uniform; a bit of an epaulette had peeped out, and the wicked fairy, Malevola, had spotted it as he went past her to the palace back door, near which she had been sitting disguised as a dog without a collar hiding from the police, and enjoying what she took to be the trouble the royal household were having with their tradesmen.

Malevola almost jumped out of her dog-skin when she saw the glitter of that epaulette.

'Hullo?' she said, and sniffed quite like a dog. 'I must look into this,' said she, and disguising herself as a toad, she crept unseen into the pipe by which the copper emptied itself into the palace moat – for of course there was a copper in one of the palace cellars as there always is in cellars in the North Country.

Now this copper had been a great trial to the decorators. If there is anything you don't like about your house, you can either try to conceal it or 'make a feature of it'. And as concealment of the copper was impossible, it was decided to 'make it a feature' by covering it with green moss and planting a tree in it, a little apple tree all in bloom. It had been very much admired.

Malevola, hastily altering her disguise to that of a mole, dug her way through the earth that the copper was full of, got to the top and put out a sharp nose just as Benevola was saying in that soft voice which Malevola always thought so affected:

'The Princess shall love and be loved all her life long.'

'So she shall,' said the wicked fairy, assuming her own shape amid the screams of the audience. 'Be quiet, you silly cuckoo,' she said to the Lord Chamberlain, whose screams were specially piercing, 'or I'll give *you* a christening present too.'

Instantly there was a dreadful silence. Only Queen Eliza, who had caught up the baby at Malevola's first word, said feebly:

'Oh, *don't*, dear Malevola.'

And the King said, 'It isn't exactly a party, don't you know. Quite informal. Just a few friends dropped in, eh, what?'

'So I perceive,' said Malevola, laughing that dreadful laugh of hers which makes other people feel as though they would never be able to laugh any more. 'Well, I've dropped in too. Let's have a look at the child.'

The poor Queen dared not refuse. She tottered forward with the baby in her arms.

'Humph!' said Malevola, 'your precious daughter will have beauty and grace and all the rest of the tuppenny-halfpenny rubbish those niminy-piminy minxes have given her. But she will be turned out of her kingdom. She will have to face her enemies without a single human being to stand by her, and she shall never come to her own again until she finds –' Malevola hesitated. She could not think of anything sufficiently unlikely – 'until she finds,' she repeated . . .

'A thousand spears to follow her to battle,' said a new voice, 'a thousand spears devoted to her and to her alone.'

A very young fairy fluttered down from the little apple tree where she had been hiding among the pink and white blossom.

'I am very young, I know,' she said apologetically, 'and I've only just finished my last course of Fairy History. So I know that if a fairy stops more than half a second in a curse she can't go on, and someone else may finish it for her. That is so, Your Majesty, isn't it?' she said, appealing to Benevola. And the Queen of the Fairies said Yes, that was the law, only it was such an old one most people had forgotten it.

'You think yourself very clever,' said Malevola, 'but as a matter of fact you're simply silly. That's the very thing I've provided against. She *can't* have anyone to stand by her in battle, so she'll lose her kingdom and everyone will be killed, and I shall come to the funeral. It will be enormous,' she added rubbing her hands at the joyous thought.

'If you've quite finished,' said the King politely, 'and if you're sure you won't take any refreshment, may I wish you a very good afternoon?' He held the door open himself, and Malevola went out chuckling. The whole of the party then burst into tears.

'Never mind,' said the King at last, wiping his eyes with the tails of his ermine. 'It's a long way off and perhaps it won't happen after all.'

But of course it did.

The King did what he could to prepare his daughter for the fight in which she was to stand alone against her enemies. He had her taught fencing and riding and shooting, both with the cross bow and the long bow, as well as with pistols, rifles, and artillery. She learned to dive and to swim, to run and to jump, to box and to wrestle, so that she grew up as strong and healthy as any young man, and could, indeed, have got the best of a fight with any prince of her own age. But the few princes who called at the palace did not come to fight the Princess, and when they heard that the Princess had no dowry except the gifts of the fairies, and also what Malevola's gift had been, they all said they had just looked in as they were passing and that they must be going now, thank you. And went.

And then the dreadful thing happened. The tradesmen, who had for years been calling for the last time before, etc., really decided to place the matter in other hands. They called in a neighbouring king who marched his army into Ozymandias's country, conquered the army – the soldiers' wages hadn't been paid for years – turned out the King and Queen, paid the tradesmen's bills, had most of the palace walls papered with the receipts, and set up housekeeping there himself.

Now when this happened the Princess was away on a visit to her aunt, the Empress of Oricalchia, half the world away, and there is no regular post between the two countries, so that when she came home, travelling with a train of fifty-four camels, which is rather slow work, and arrived at her own kingdom, she expected to find all the flags flying and the bells ringing and the streets decked in roses to welcome her home.

Instead of which nothing of the kind. The streets were all as dull as dull, the shops were closed because it was early-closing day, and she did not see a single person she knew.

She left the fifty-four camels laden with the presents her aunt had given her outside the gates, and rode alone on her own pet camel to the palace, wondering whether perhaps her father had not received the letter she had sent on ahead by carrier pigeon the day before.

And when she got to the palace and got off her camel and went in, there was a strange king on her father's throne and a strange queen sat in her mother's place at his side.

'Where's my father?' said the Princess, bold as brass, standing on the steps of the throne. 'And what are you doing there?'

'I might ask you that,' said the King. 'Who are you, anyway?'

'I am the Princess Ozyliza,' said she.

'Oh, I've heard of you,' said the King. 'You've been expected for some time. Your father's been evicted, so now you know. No, I can't give you his address.'

Just then someone came and whispered to the Queen that fifty-four camels laden with silks and velvets and monkeys and parakeets and the richest treasures of Oricalchia were outside the city gate. She put two and two together, and whispered to the King, who nodded and said:

'I wish to make a new law.'

Everyone fell flat on his face. The law is so much respected in that country.

'No one called Ozyliza is allowed to own property in this kingdom,' said the King. 'Turn out that stranger.'

So the Princess was turned out of her father's palace, and went out and cried in the palace gardens where she had been so happy when she was little.

And the baker's boy, who was now the baker's young man, came by with the standard bread and saw some one crying among the oleanders, and went to say, 'Cheer up!' to whoever it was. And it was the Princess. He knew her at once.

'Oh, Princess,' he said, 'cheer up! Nothing is ever so bad as it seems.'

'Oh, Baker's Boy,' said she, for she knew him too, 'how can I cheer up? I am turned out of my kingdom. I haven't got my father's address, and I have to face my enemies without a single human being to stand by me.'

'That's not true, at any rate,' said the baker's boy, whose name was Erinaceus, 'you've got me. If you'll let me be your squire, I'll follow you round the world and help you to fight your enemies.'

'You won't be let,' said the Princess sadly, 'but I thank you very much all the same.'

She dried her eyes and stood up.

'I must go,' she said, 'and I've nowhere to go to.'

Now as soon as the Princess had been turned out of the palace, the Queen said, 'You'd much better have beheaded her for treason.' And the King said, 'I'll tell the archers to pick her off as she leaves the grounds.'

So when she stood up, out there among the oleanders, some one on the terrace cried, 'There she is!' and instantly a flight of winged arrows crossed the garden. At the cry Erinaceus flung himself in front of her, clasping her in his arms and turning his back to the arrows. The Royal Archers were a thousand strong and all excellent shots. Erinaceus felt a thousand arrows sticking into his back.

'And now my last friend is dead,' cried the Princess. But being a very strong princess, she dragged him into the shrubbery out of sight of the palace, and then dragged him into the wood and called aloud on Benevola, Queen of the Fairies, and Benevola came.

'They've killed my only friend,' said the Princess, 'at least . . . Shall I pull out the arrows?'

'If you do,' said the Fairy, 'he'll certainly bleed to death.'

'And he'll die if they stay in,' said the Princess.

'Not necessarily,' said the Fairy; 'let me cut them a little shorter.' She did, with her fairy pocket-knife. 'Now,' she said, 'I'll do what I can, but I'm afraid it'll be a disappointment to you both. Erinaceus,' she went on, addressing the unconscious baker's boy with the stumps of the arrows still sticking in him, 'I command you, as soon as I have vanished, to assume the form of a hedge-pig. The hedge-pig', she exclaimed to the Princess, 'is the only nice person who can live comfortably with a thousand spikes sticking out of him. Yes, I know there are porcupines, but porcupines are vicious and ill-mannered. Goodbye!'

And with that she vanished. So did Erinaceus,

and the Princess found herself alone among the oleanders; and on the green turf was a small and very prickly brown hedge-pig. 'Oh, dear!' she said, 'now I'm all alone again, and the baker's boy has given his life for mine, and mine isn't worth having.'

'It's worth more than all the world,' said a sharp little voice at her feet.

'Oh, can you talk?' she said, quite cheered.

'Why not?' said the hedge-pig sturdily; 'it's only the *form* of the hedge-pig I've assumed. I'm Erinaceus inside, all right enough. Pick me up in a corner of your mantle so as not to prick your darling hands.'

'You mustn't call names, you know,' said the Princess, 'even your hedge-pigginess can't excuse such liberties.'

'I'm sorry, Princess,' said the hedge-pig, 'but I can't help it. Only human beings speak lies; all other creatures tell the truth. Now I've got a hedge-pig's tongue it won't speak anything but the truth. And the truth is that I love you more than all the world.'

'Well,' said the Princess thoughtfully, 'since you're a hedge-pig I suppose you may love me, and I may love you. Like pet dogs or goldfish. Dear little hedge-pig, then!'

'Don't!' said the hedge-pig, 'remember I'm the baker's boy in my mind and soul. My hedge-pigginess is only skin-deep. Pick me up, dearest of Princesses, and let us go to seek our fortunes.'

'I think it's my parents I ought to seek,' said the Princess. 'However . . .'

She picked up the hedge-pig in the corner of her mantle and they went away through the wood.

They slept that night at a wood-cutter's cottage. The wood-cutter was very kind, and made a nice little box of beech-wood for the hedge-pig to be carried in, and he told the Princess that most of her father's subjects were still loyal, but that no one could fight for him because they would be fighting for the Princess too, and however much they might wish to do this, Malevola's curse assured them that it was impossible.

So the Princess put her hedge-pig in its little box and went on, looking everywhere for her father and mother, and, after more adventures than I have time to tell you, she found them at last, living in quite a poor way in a semi-detached villa at Tooting. They were very glad to see her, but when they heard that she meant to try to get back the kingdom, the King said:

'I shouldn't bother, my child, I really shouldn't. We are quite happy here. I have the pension always given to Deposed Monarchs, and your mother is becoming a really economical manager.'

The Queen blushed with pleasure, and said, 'Thank you, dear. But if you should succeed in turning that wicked usurper out, Ozyliza, I hope I shall be a better queen than I used to be. I am learning housekeeping at an evening class at the Crown-maker's Institute.'

The Princess kissed her parents and went out into the garden to think it over. But the garden was small and quite full of wet washing hung on lines. So she went into the road, but that was full of dust and perambulators. Even the wet washing was better than that, so she went back and sat down on the grass in a white alley of tablecloths and sheets, all marked with a crown in indelible ink. And she took the hedge-pig out of the box. It was rolled up in a ball, but she stroked the little bit of soft forehead that you can always find if you look carefully at a rolled-up hedge-pig, and the hedge-pig uncurled and said:

'I am afraid I was asleep, Princess dear. Did you want me?'

'You're the only person who knows all about everything,' said she. 'I haven't told father and mother about the arrows. Now what do you advise?'

Erinaceus was flattered at having his advice asked, but unfortunately he hadn't any to give.

'It's your work, Princess,' he said. 'I can only promise to do anything a hedge-pig *can* do. It's not much. Of course I could die for you, but that's so useless.'

'Quite,' said she.

'I wish I were invisible,' he said dreamily.

'Oh, where are you?' cried Ozyliza, for the hedge-pig had vanished.

'Here,' said a sharp little voice. 'You can't see me, but I can see everything I want to see. And I can see what to do. I'll crawl into my box, and you must disguise yourself as an old French governess with the best references and answer the advertisement that the wicked king put yesterday in the *Usurpers Journal*.'

The Queen helped the Princess to disguise herself, which, of course, the Queen would never have done if she had known about the arrows; and the King gave her some of his pension to buy a ticket with, so she went back quite quickly, by train, to her own kingdom.

The usurping King at once engaged the French governess to teach his cook to read French cookery books, because the best recipes are in French. Of course he had no idea that there was a princess, *the* Princess, beneath the governessial disguise. The French lessons were from 6 to 8 in the morning and from 2 to 4 in the afternoon, and all the rest of the time the governess could spend as she liked. She spent it walking about the palace gardens and talking to her invisible hedge-pig. They talked about everything under the sun, and the hedge-pig was the best of company.

'How did you become invisible?' she asked one day, and it said, 'I suppose it was Benevola's doing. Only I think everyone gets *one* wish granted if they only wish hard enough.'

On the fifty-fifth day the hedge-pig said, 'Now, Princess dear, I'm going to begin to get you back your kingdom.'

And next morning the King came down to

breakfast in a dreadful rage with his face covered up in bandages.

'This palace is haunted,' he said. 'In the middle of the night a dreadful spiked ball was thrown in my face. I lighted a match. There was nothing.'

The Queen said, 'Nonsense! You must have been dreaming.'

But next morning it was her turn to come down with a bandaged face. And the night after, the King had the spiky ball thrown at him again. And then the Queen had it. And then they both had it, so that they couldn't sleep at all, and had to lie awake with nothing to think of but their wickedness. And every five minutes a very little voice whispered:

'Who stole the kingdom? Who killed the Princess?' till the King and Queen could have screamed with misery.

And at last the Queen said, 'We needn't have killed the Princess.'

And the King said, 'I've been thinking that, too.'

And next day the King said, 'I don't know that we ought to have taken this kingdom. We had a really high-class kingdom of our own.'

'I've been thinking that too,' said the Queen.

By this time their hands and arms and necks and faces and ears were very sore indeed, and they were sick with want of sleep.

'Look here,' said the King, 'let's chuck it. Let's write to Ozymandias and tell him he can take over his kingdom again. I've had jolly well enough of this.'

'Let's,' said the Queen, 'but we can't bring the Princess to life again. I do wish we could,' and she cried a little through her bandages into her egg, for it was breakfast time.

'Do you mean that?' said a little sharp voice, though there was no one to be seen in the room. The King and Queen clung to each other in terror, upsetting the urn over the toast-rack.

'Do you mean it?' said the voice again; 'answer, yes or no.'

'Yes,' said the Queen, 'I don't know who you are, but, yes, yes, yes. I can't *think* how we could have been so wicked.'

'Nor I,' said the King.

'Then send for the French governess,' said the voice.

'Ring the bell, dear,' said the Queen. 'I'm sure what it says is right. It is the voice of conscience. I've often heard *of* it, but I never heard it before.'

The King pulled the richly jewelled bell-rope and ten magnificent green and gold footmen appeared.

'Please ask Mademoiselle to step this way,' said the Queen.

The ten magnificent green and gold footmen found the governess beside the marble basin feeding the gold-fish, and, bowing their ten green backs, they gave the Queen's message. The governess who, everyone agreed, was always most obliging, went at once to the pink satin breakfast-room where the King and Queen were sitting, almost unrecognizable in their bandages.

'Yes, Your Majesties?' said she curtseying.

'The voice of conscience', said the Queen, 'told us to send for you. Is there any recipe in the French books for bringing shot princesses to life? If so, will you kindly translate it for us?'

'There *is one,*' said the Princess thoughtfully, 'and it is quite simple. Take a king and a queen and the voice of conscience. Place them in a clean pink breakfast-room with eggs, coffee, and toast. Add a full-sized French governess. The king and queen must be thoroughly pricked and bandaged, and the voice of conscience must be very distinct.'

'Is that all?' asked the Queen.

'That's all,' said the governess, 'except that the king and queen must have two more bandages over their eyes, and keep them on till the voice of conscience has counted fifty-five very slowly.'

'If you would be so kind,' said the Queen, 'as to bandage us with our table napkins? Only be careful how you fold them, because our faces are very sore, and the royal monogram is very stiff and hard owing to its being embroidered in seed pearls by special command.'

'I will be very careful,' said the governess kindly.

The moment the King and Queen were blindfolded, the 'voice of conscience' began, 'one, two, three,' and Ozyliza tore off her disguise, and under the fussy black-and-violet-spotted alpaca of the French governess was the simple slim cloth-of-silver dress of the Princess. She stuffed the alpaca up the chimney and the grey wig into the tea-cosy, and had disposed of the mittens in the coffee-pot and the elastic-side boots in the coal-scuttle, just as the voice of conscience said:

'Fifty-three, fifty-four, fifty-five!' and stopped.

The King and Queen pulled off the bandages, and there, alive and well, with bright clear eyes and pinky cheeks and a mouth that smiled, was the Princess whom they supposed to have been killed by the thousand arrows of their thousand archers.

Before they had time to say a word the Princess said:

'Good morning, Your Majesties. I am afraid you have had bad dreams. So have I. Let us all try to forget them. I hope you will stay a little longer in my palace. You are very welcome. I am so sorry you have been hurt.'

'We deserved it,' said the Queen, 'and we want to say we have heard the voice of conscience, and do please forgive us.'

'Not another word,' said the Princess, '*do* let me have some fresh tea made. And some more eggs. These are quite cold. And the urn's upset. We'll have a new breakfast. And I *am* so sorry your faces are so sore.'

'If you kissed them,' said the voice which the

King and Queen called the voice of conscience, 'their faces would not be sore any more.'

'May I?' said Ozyliza, and kissed the King's ear and the Queen's nose, all she could get at through the bandages.

And instantly they were quite well.

They had a delightful breakfast. Then the King caused the royal household to assemble in the throne-room, and there announced that, as the Princess had come to claim the kingdom, they were returning to their own kingdom by the three-seventeen train on Thursday.

Everyone cheered like mad, and the whole town was decorated and illuminated that evening. Flags flew from every house, and the bells all rang, just as the Princess had expected them to do that day when she came home with the fifty-five camels. All the treasure these had carried was given back to the Princess, and the camels themselves were restored to her, hardly at all the worse for wear.

The usurping King and Queen were seen off at the station by the Princess, and parted from her with real affection. You see they weren't completely wicked in their hearts, but they had never had time to think before. And being kept awake at night forced them to think. And the 'voice of conscience' gave them something to think about.

They gave the Princess the receipted bills, with which most of the palace was papered, in return for board and lodging.

When they were gone a telegram was sent off.

Ozymandias Rex, Esq.,
Chatsworth,
Delamere Road,
Tooting,
England.

Please come home at once. Palace vacant. Tenants have left. – OZYLIZA P.

And they came immediately.

When they arrived the Princess told them the whole story, and they kissed and praised her, and called her their deliverer and the saviour of her country.

'*I* haven't done anything,' she said. 'It was Erinaceus who did everything and –'

'But the fairies said', interrupted the King, who was never clever at the best of times, 'that you couldn't get the kingdom back till you had a thousand spears devoted to you, to you alone.'

'There are a thousand spears in my back,' said a little sharp voice, 'and they are all devoted to the Princess and to her alone.'

'Don't!' said the King irritably. 'That voice coming out of nothing makes me jump.'

'I can't get used to it either,' said the Queen. 'We must have a gold cage built for the little animal. But I must say I wish it was visible.'

'So do I,' said the Princess earnestly. And instantly it was. I suppose the Princess wished it very hard, for there was the hedge-pig with its long spiky body and its little pointed face, and its bright eyes, its small round ears, and its sharp, turned-up nose.

It looked at the Princess but it did not speak.

'Say something *now*,' said Queen Eliza. 'I should like to *see* a hedge-pig speak.'

'The truth is, if speak I must, I must speak the truth,' said Erinaceus. 'The Princess has thrown away her life-wish to make me visible. I wish she had wished instead for something nice for herself.'

'Oh, was that my life-wish?' cried the Princess. 'I didn't know, dear hedge-pig, I didn't know. If I'd only known, I would have wished you back into your proper shape.'

'If you had,' said the hedge-pig, 'it would have been the shape of a dead man. Remember that I have a thousand spears in my back, and no man can carry those and live.'

The Princess burst into tears.

'Oh, you can't go on being a hedge-pig for ever,' she said, 'it's not fair. I can't bear it. Oh Mamma! Oh Papa! Oh Benevola!'

And there stood Benevola before them, a little dazzling figure with blue butterfly's wings and a wreath of moonshine.

'Well?' she said, 'well?'

'Oh, you know,' said the Princess, still crying. 'I've thrown away my life-wish, and he's still a hedge-pig. Can't you do *anything*?'

'*I* can't,' said the Fairy, 'but you can. Your kisses are magic kisses. Don't you remember how you cured the King and Queen of all the wounds the hedge-pig made by rolling itself on to their faces in the night?'

'But she can't go kissing hedge-pigs,' said the Queen, 'it would be most unsuitable. Besides it would hurt her.'

But the hedge-pig raised its little pointed face, and the Princess took it up in her hands. She had long since learned how to do this without hurting either herself or it. She looked in its little bright eyes.

'I would kiss you on every one of your thousand spears,' she said, 'to give you what you wish.'

'Kiss me once', it said, 'where my fur is soft. That is all I wish, and enough to live and die for.'

She stooped her head and kissed it on its forehead where the fur is soft, just where the prickles begin.

And instantly she was standing with her hands on a young man's shoulders and her lips on a young man's face just where the hair begins and the forehead leaves off. And all round his feet lay a pile of fallen arrows.

She drew back and looked at him.

'Erinaceus,' she said, 'you're different – from the baker's boy I mean.'

'When I was an invisible hedge-pig,' he said, 'I knew everything. Now I have forgotten all that wisdom save only two things. One is that I am a king's son. I was stolen away in infancy by an unprincipled baker, and I am really the son of that usurping King whose face I rolled on in the night. It is a painful thing to roll on your father's face when you are all spiky, but I did it, Princess, for your sake, and for my father's too. And now I will go to him and tell him all, and ask his forgiveness.'

'You won't go away?' said the Princess. 'Ah! don't go away. What shall I do without my hedge-pig?'

Erinaceus stood still, looking very handsome and like a prince.

'What is the other thing that you remember of your hedge-pig wisdom?' asked the Queen curiously. And Erinaceus answered, not to her but to the Princess:

'The other thing, Princess, is that I love you.'

'Isn't there a third thing, Erinaceus?' said the Princess, looking down.

'There is, but you must speak that, not I.'

'Oh,' said the Princess, a little disappointed, 'then you knew that I loved you?'

'Hedge-pigs are very wise little beasts,' said Erinaceus, 'but I only knew that when you told it me.'

'I – told you?'

'When you kissed my little pointed face, Princess,' said Erinaceus, 'I knew then.'

'My goodness gracious me,' said the King.

'Quite so,' said Benevola, 'and I wouldn't ask *anyone* to the wedding.'

'Except you, dear,' said the Queen.

'Well, as I happened to be passing . . . there's no time like the present,' said Benevola briskly. 'Suppose you give orders for the wedding bells to be rung now, at once!'

5

SEPTIMUS SEPTIMUSSON

The wind was screaming over the marsh. It shook the shutters and rattled the windows, and the little boy lay awake in the bare attic. His mother came softly up the ladder stairs shading the flame of the tallow candle with her hand.

'I'm not asleep, mother,' said he. And she heard the tears in his voice.

'Why, silly lad,' she said, sitting down on the straw-bed beside him and putting the candle on the floor, 'what are you crying for?'

'It's the wind keeps calling me, mother,' he said. 'It won't let me alone. It never has since I put up the little weather-cock for it to play with. It keeps saying, "Wake up, Septimus Septimusson, wake up, you're the seventh son of a seventh son. You can see the fairies and hear the beasts speak, and you must go out and seek your fortune." And I'm afraid, and I don't want to go.'

'I should think not indeed,' said his mother. 'The wind doesn't talk, Sep, not really. You just go to sleep like a good boy, and I'll get father to bring you a gingerbread pig from the fair tomorrow.'

But Sep lay awake a long time listening to what the wind really did keep on saying, and feeling ashamed to think how frightened he was of going out all alone to seek his fortune – a thing all the boys in books were only too happy to do.

Next evening father brought home the loveliest gingerbread pig with currant eyes. Sep ate it, and it made him less anxious than ever to go out into the world where, perhaps, no one would give him gingerbread pigs ever any more.

Before he went to bed he ran down to the shore where a great new harbour was being made. The workmen had been blasting the big rocks, and on one of the rocks a lot of mussels were sticking. He stood looking at them, and then suddenly he heard a lot of little voices crying, 'Oh Sep, we're so frightened, we're choking.'

The voices were thin and sharp as the edges of mussel shells. They were indeed the voices of the mussels themselves.

'Oh dear,' said Sep, 'I'm so sorry, but I can't move the rock back into the sea, you know. Can I now?'

'No,' said the mussels, 'but if you speak to the wind – you know his language and he's very fond of you since you made that toy for him, – he'll blow the sea up till the waves wash us back into deep water.'

'But I'm afraid of the wind,' said Sep, 'it says things that frighten me.'

'Oh, very well,' said the mussels, 'we don't want you to be afraid. We can die all right if necessary.'

Then Sep shivered and trembled.

'Go away,' said the thin sharp voices. 'We'll die – but we'd rather die in our own brave company.'

'I know I'm a coward,' said Sep. 'Oh, wait a minute.'

'Death won't wait,' said the little voices.

'I can't speak to the wind, I won't,' said Sep, and almost at the same moment he heard himself call out, 'Oh wind, please come and blow up the waves to save the poor mussels.'

The wind answered with a boisterous shout:

'All right, my boy,' it shrieked, 'I'm coming.' And come it did. And when it had attended to the mussels it came and whispered to Sep in his attic. And to his great surprise, instead of covering his head with the bed-clothes, as usual, and trying not to listen, he found himself sitting up in bed and talking to the wind, man to man.

'Why,' he said, 'I'm not afraid of you any more.'

'Of course not, we're friends now,' said the wind. 'That's because we joined together to do a kindness to someone. There's nothing like that for making people friends.'

'Oh,' said Sep.

'Yes,' said the wind, 'and now, old chap, when will you go out and seek your fortune? Remember how poor your father is, and the fortune, if you find it, won't be just for you, but for your father and mother and the others.'

'Oh,' said Sep, 'I didn't think of that.'

'Yes,' said the wind, 'really, my dear fellow, I do hate to bother you, but it's better to fix a time. Now when shall we start?'

'We?' said Sep. 'Are you going with me?'

'I'll see you a bit of the way,' said the wind. 'What do you say now? Shall we start tonight? There's no time like the present.'

'I do hate going,' said Sep.

'Of course you do!' said the wind, cordially. 'Come along. Get into your things, and we'll make a beginning.'

So Sep dressed, and he wrote on his slate in very big letters, 'Gone to seek our fortune,' and he put it on the table so that his mother should see it when she came down in the morning. And he went out of the cottage and the wind kindly shut the door after him.

The wind gently pushed him down to the shore, and there he got into his father's boat, which was called the *Septimus and Susie*, after his father and mother, and the wind carried him across to another country and there he landed.

'Now,' said the wind, clapping him on the back, 'off you go, and good luck to you!'

And it turned round and took the boat home again.

When Sep's mother found the writing on the slate, and his father found the boat gone they feared that Sep was drowned, but when the wind brought the boat back wrong way up, they were quite sure, and they both cried for many a long day.

The wind tried to tell them that Sep was all right, but they couldn't understand wind-talk, and they only said, 'Drat the wind,' and fastened the shutters up tight, and put wedges in the windows.

Sep walked along the straight white road that led across the new country. He had no more idea how to look for *his* fortune than you would have if you suddenly left off reading this and went out of your front door to seek *yours*.

However, he had made a start, and that is always something. When he had gone exactly seven miles on that straight foreign road, between strange trees, and bordered with flowers he did not know the names of, he heard a groaning in the wood, and someone sighing and saying, 'Oh, how hard it is, to have to die and never see my wife and the little cubs again.'

The voice was rough as a lion's mane, and strong as a lion's claws, and Sep was very frightened. But he said, 'I'm not afraid,' and then oddly enough he found he had spoken the truth – he wasn't afraid.

He broke through the bushes and found that the person who had spoken was indeed a lion. A javelin had pierced its shoulder and fastened it to a great tree.

'All right,' cried Sep, 'hold still a minute, sir.'

He got out his knife and cut and cut at the shaft of the javelin till he was able to break it off. Then the lion drew back and the broken shaft passed through the wound and the broken javelin was left sticking in the tree.

'I'm really extremely obliged, my dear fellow,' said the lion warmly. 'Pray command me, if there's any little thing I can do for you at any time.'

'Don't mention it,' said Sep with proper politeness, 'delighted to have been of use to you, I'm sure.'

So they parted. As Sep scrambled through the bushes back to the road he kicked against an axe that lay on the ground.

'Hullo,' said he, 'some poor woodman's dropped this, and not been able to find it. I'll take it along – perhaps I may meet him.'

He was getting very tired and very hungry, and presently he sat down to rest under a chestnut-tree, and he heard two little voices talking in the branches, voices soft as a squirrel's fur, and bright as a squirrel's eyes. They were, indeed, the voices of two squirrels.

'Hush,' said one, 'there's someone below.'

'Oh,' said the other, 'it's a horrid boy. Let's scurry away.'

'I'm not a horrid boy,' said Sep. 'I'm the seventh son of a seventh son.'

'Oh,' said Mrs Squirrel, 'of course that makes all the difference. Have some nuts?'

'Rather,' said Sep. 'At least I mean, yes, if you please.'

So the squirrels brought nuts down to him, and when he had eaten as many as he wanted they filled his pockets, and then in return he chopped all the lower boughs off the chestnut-tree, so that boys who were *not* seventh sons could not climb up and interfere with the squirrels' housekeeping arrangements.

Then they parted, the best of friends, and Sep went on.

'I haven't found my fortune yet,' said he, 'but I've made a friend or two.'

And just as he was saying that, he turned a corner of the road and met an old gentleman in a fur-lined coat riding a fine, big, grey horse.

'Hullo!' said the gentleman. 'Who are you, and where are you off to so bright and early?'

'I'm Septimus Septimusson,' said Sep, 'and I'm going to seek my fortune.'

'And you've taken an axe to help you carve your way to glory?'

'No,' said Sep, 'I found it, and I suppose someone lost it. So I'm bringing it along in case I meet him.'

'Heavy, isn't it?' said the old gentleman.

'Yes,' said Sep.

'Then I'll carry it for you,' said the old gentleman, 'for it's one that my head forester lost yesterday. And now come along with me, for you're the boy I've been looking for for seven years – an honest boy and the seventh son of a seventh son.'

So Sep went home with the gentleman, who was a great lord in that country, and he lived in that lord's castle and was taught everything that a gentleman ought to know. And in return he told the lord all about the ways of birds and beasts – for as he understood their talk he knew more about them than anyone else in that country. And the lord wrote it all down in a book, and half the people said it was wonderfully clever, and the other half said it was nonsense, and how could he know. This was fame, and the lord was very pleased. But though the old lord was so famous he would not leave his castle, for he had a hump that an enchanter had fastened on to him, and he couldn't bear to be seen with it.

'But you'll get rid of it for me some day, my boy,' he used to say. 'No one but the seventh son of a seventh son and an honest boy can do it. So all the doctors say.'

So Sep grew up. And when he was twenty-one – straight as a lance and handsome as a picture – the old lord said to him:

'My boy, you've been like a son to me, but now it's time you got married and had sons of your own. Is there any girl you'd like to marry?'

'No,' said Sep, 'I never did care much for girls.'

The old lord laughed.

'Then you must set out again and seek your fortune once more,' he said, 'because no man has really found his fortune till he's found the lady who is his heart's lady. Choose the best horse in the stable, and off you go, lad, and my blessing go with you.'

So Sep chose a good red horse and set out, and he rode straight to the great city, that shone golden across the plain, and when he got there he found everyone crying.

'Why, whatever is the matter?' said Sep, reining in the red horse in front of a smithy, where the apprentices were crying on to the fires, and the smith was dropping tears on the anvil.

'Why, the Princess is dying,' said the blacksmith blowing his nose. 'A nasty, wicked magician – he had a spite against the King, and he got at the Princess when she was playing ball in the garden, and now she's blind and deaf and dumb. And she won't eat.'

'And she'll die,' said the first apprentice.

'And she *is* such a dear,' said the other apprentice.

Sep sat still on the red horse thinking.

'Has anything been done?' he asked.

'Oh yes,' said the blacksmith. 'All the doctors have seen her, but they can't do anything. And the King has advertised in the usual way, that anyone who can cure her may marry her. But it's no good. King's sons aren't what they used to be. A silly lot they are nowadays, all taken up with football and cricket and golf.'

'Humph,' said Sep, 'thank you. Which is the way to the palace?'

The blacksmith pointed, and then burst into tears again. Sep rode on.

When he got to the palace he asked to see the King. Everyone there was crying too, from the footman who opened the door to the King, who was sitting upon his golden throne and looking at his fine collection of butterflies through floods of tears.

'Oh dear me yes, young man,' said the King, 'you may *see* her and welcome, but it's no good.'

'We can but try,' said Sep. So he was taken to the room where the Princess sat huddled up on her silver throne among the white velvet cushions with her crown all on one side, crying out of her poor blind eyes, so that the tears ran down over her green gown with the red roses on it.

And directly he saw her he knew that she was the only girl, Princess as she was, with a crown and a throne, who could ever be his heart's lady. He went up to her and kneeled at her side and took her hand and kissed it. The Princess started. She could not see or hear him, but at the touch of his hand and his lips she knew that he was her heart's lord, and she threw her arms round his neck, and cried more than ever.

He held her in his arms and stroked her hair till she stopped crying, and then he called for bread and milk. This was brought in a silver basin, and he fed her with it as you feed a little child.

The news ran through the city, 'The Princess has eaten,' and all the bells were set ringing. Sep said goodnight to his Princess and went to bed in the best bedroom of the palace. Early in the grey morning he got up and leaned out of the open window and called to his old friend the wind.

And the wind came bustling in and clapped him on the back, crying, 'Well, my boy, and what can I do for you? Eh?'

Sep told him all about the Princess.

'Well,' said the wind, 'you've not done so badly. At any rate you've got her love. And you couldn't have got that with anybody's help but your own. Now, of course, the thing to do is to find the wicked Magician.'

'Of course,' said Sep.

'Well – I travel a good deal – I'll keep my eyes open, and let you know if I hear anything.'

Sep spent the day holding the Princess's hand, and feeding her at meal times; and that night the wind rattled his window and said, 'Let me in.'

It came in very noisily, and said, 'Well, I've found your Magician, he's in the forest pretending to be a mole.'

'How can I find him?' said Sep.

'Haven't you any friends in the forest?' asked the wind.

Then Sep remembered his friends the squirrels, and he mounted his horse and rode away to the chestnut-tree where they lived. They were charmed to see him grown so tall and strong and handsome, and when he had told them his story they said at once:

'Oh yes! delighted to be of any service to you.' And they called to all their little brothers and cousins, and uncles and nephews to search the forest for a mole that wasn't really a mole, and quite soon they found him, and hustled and shoved him along till he was face to face with Sep, in a green glade. The glade was green, but all the bushes and trees around were red-brown with squirrel fur, and shining bright with squirrel eyes.

Then Sep said, 'Give the Princess back her eyes and her hearing and her voice.'

But the mole would not.

'Give the Princess back her eyes and her hearing and her voice,' said Sep again. But the mole only gnashed his wicked teeth and snarled.

And then in a minute the squirrels fell on the mole and killed it, and Sep thanked them and rode back to the palace, for, of course, he knew that when a magician is killed, all his magic un-works itself instantly.

But when he got to his Princess she was still as deaf as a post and as dumb as a stone, and she was still crying bitterly with her poor blind eyes, till the tears ran down her grass-green gown with the red roses on it.

'Cheer up, my sweetheart,' he said, though he knew she couldn't hear him, and as he spoke the wind came in at the open window, and spoke very softly, because it was in the presence of the Princess.

'All right,' it whispered, 'the old villain gave us

the slip that journey. Got out of the mole-skin in the very nick of time. He's a wild boar now.'

'Come,' said Sep, fingering his sword-hilt, 'I'll kill that myself without asking it any questions.'

So he went and fought it. But it was a most uncommon boar, as big as a horse, with tusks half a yard long; and although Sep wounded it it jerked the sword out of his hand with its tusk, and was just going to trample him out of life with its hard, heavy pig's feet, when a great roar sounded through the forest.

'Ah! would ye?' said the lion, and fastened teeth and claws in the great boar's back. The boar turned with a scream of rage, but the lion had got a good grip, and it did not loosen teeth or claws till the boar lay quiet.

'Is he dead?' asked Sep when he came to himself.

'Oh yes, he's *dead* right enough,' said the lion; but the wind came up puffing and blowing, and said:

'It's no good, he's got away again, and now he's a fish. I was just a minute too late to see *what* fish. An old oyster told me about it, only he hadn't the wit to notice what particular fish the scoundrel changed into.'

So then Sep went back to the palace, and he said to the King:

'Let me marry the dear Princess, and we'll go out and seek our fortune. I've got to kill that Magician, and I'll do it too, or my name's not

Septimus Septimusson. But it may take years and years, and I can't be away from the Princess all that time, because she won't eat unless I feed her. You see the difficulty, Sire?'

The King saw it. And that very day Sep was married to the Princess in her green gown with the red roses on it, and they set out together.

The wind went with them, and the wind, or something else, seemed to say to Sep, 'Go home, take your wife home to your mother.'

So he did. He crossed the land and he crossed the sea, and he went up the red-brick path to his father's cottage, and he peeped in at the door and said:

'Father, mother, here's my wife.'

They were so pleased to see him – for they had thought him dead, that they didn't notice the Princess at first, and when they did notice her they wondered at her beautiful face and her beautiful gown – but it wasn't till they had all settled down to supper – boiled rabbit it was – and they noticed Sep feeding his wife as one feeds a baby that they saw that she was blind.

And then all the story had to be told.

'Well, well,' said the fisherman, 'you and your wife bide here with us. I daresay I'll catch that old sinner in my nets one of these fine days.' But he never did. And Sep and his wife lived with the old people. And they were happy after a fashion – but of an evening Sep used to wander and wonder, and wonder and wander by the sea-shore, wondering as he wandered whether he wouldn't ever have the luck to catch that fish.

And one evening as he wandered wondering he heard a little, sharp, thin voice say:

'Sep, I've got it.'

'What?' asked Sep, forgetting his manners.

'I've got it,' said a big mussel on a rock close by him, 'the magic stone that the Magician does his enchantments with. He dropped it out of his mouth and I shut my shells on it – and now he's sweeping up and down the sea like a mad fish, looking for it – for he knows he can never change into anything else unless he gets it back. Here, take the nasty thing, it's making me feel quite ill.'

It opened its shells wide, and Sep saw a pearl. He reached out his hand and took it.

'That's better,' said the mussel, washing its shells out with salt water.

'Can *I* do magic with it?' Sep eagerly asked.

'No,' said the mussel sadly, 'it's of no use to anyone but the owner. Now, if I were you, I'd get into a boat, and if your friend the wind will help us, I believe we really can do the trick.'

'I'm at your service, of course,' said the wind, getting up instantly.

The mussel whispered to the wind, who rushed off at once; and Sep launched his boat.

'Now,' said the mussel, 'you get into the very middle of the sea – or as near as you can guess it. The wind will warn all the other fishes.' As he spoke he disappeared in the dark waters.

Sep got the boat into the middle of the sea – as near as he could guess it – and waited.

After a long time he saw something swirling about in a sort of whirlpool about a hundred yards from his boat, but when he tried to move the boat towards it her bows ran on to something hard.

'Keep still, keep still, keep still,' cried thousands and thousands of sharp, thin, little voices. 'You'll kill us if you move.'

Then he looked over the boat side, and saw that the hard something was nothing but thousands and thousands of mussels all jammed close together, and through the clear water more and more were coming and piling themselves together. Almost at once his boat was slowly lifted – the top of the mussel heap showed through the water, and there he was, high and dry on a mussel reef.

And in all that part of the sea the water was disappearing, and as far as the eye could reach stretched a great plain of purple and grey – the shells of countless mussels.

Only at one spot there was still a splashing.

Then a mussel opened its shell and spoke.

'We've got him,' it said. 'We've piled ourselves up till we've filled this part of the sea. The wind warned all the good fishes – and we've got the old traitor in a little pool over there. Get out and walk over our backs – we'll all lie sideways so as not to hurt you. You must catch the fish – but whatever you do don't kill it till we give the word.'

Sep promised, and he got out and walked over the mussels to the pool, and when he saw the wicked soul of the Magician looking out through the round eyes of a big finny fish he remembered all that his Princess had suffered, and he longed to draw his sword and kill the wicked thing then and there.

But he remembered his promise. He threw a net about it, and dragged it back to the boat.

The mussels dispersed and let the boat down again into the water – and he rowed home, towing the evil fish in the net by a line.

He beached the boat, and looked along the shore. The shore looked a very odd colour. And well it might, for every bit of the sand was covered with purple-grey mussels. They had all come up out of the sea – leaving just one little bit of real yellow sand for him to beach the boat on.

'Now,' said millions of sharp thin little voices, 'Kill him, kill him!'

Sep drew his sword and waded into the shallow surf and killed the evil fish with one strong stroke.

Then such a shout went up all along the shore as that shore had never heard; and all along the shore where the mussels had been, stood men in armour and men in smock-frocks and men in leather aprons and huntsmen's coats and women and children – a whole nation of people. Close by the boat stood a King and Queen with crowns upon their heads.

'Thank you, Sep,' said the King, 'you've saved

us all. I am the King Mussel, doomed to be a mussel so long as that wretch lived. You have set us all free. And look!'

Down the path from the shore came running his own Princess, who hung round his neck crying his name and looking at him with the most beautiful eyes in the world.

'Come,' said the Mussel King, 'we have no son. You shall be our son and reign after us.'

'Thank you,' said Sep, 'but *this* is my father,' and he presented the old fisherman to His Majesty.

'Then let him come with us,' said the King royally, 'he can help me reign, or fish in the palace lake, whichever he prefers.'

'Thankee,' said Sep's father, 'I'll come and fish.'

'Your mother too,' said the Mussel Queen, kissing Sep's mother.

'Ah,' said Sep's mother, 'you're a lady, every inch. I'll go to the world's end with you.'

So they all went back by way of the foreign country where Sep had found his Princess, and they called on the old lord. He had lost his hump, and they easily persuaded him to come with them.

'You can help me reign if you like, or we have a nice book or two in the palace library,' said the Mussel King.

'Thank you,' said the old lord, 'I'll come and be your librarian if I may. Reigning isn't at all in my line.'

Then they went on to Sep's father-in-law, and when he saw how happy they all were together he said:

'Bless my beard but I've half a mind to come with you.'

'Come along,' said the Mussel King, 'you shall help me reign if you like . . . or . . .'

'No, thank you,' said the other King very quickly, 'I've had enough of reigning. My kingdom can buy a President and be a republic if it likes. I'm going to catch butterflies.'

And so he does, most happily, up to this very minute.

And Sep and his dear Princess are as happy as they deserve to be. Some people say we are all as happy as we deserve to be – but I am not sure.

6

THE WHITE CAT

The White Cat lived at the back of a shelf at the darkest end of the inside attic which was nearly dark all over. It had lived there for years, because one of its white china ears was chipped, so that it was no longer a possible ornament for the spare bedroom.

Tavy found it at the climax of a wicked and glorious afternoon. He had been left alone. The servants were the only other people in the house. He had promised to be good. He had meant to be good. And he had not been. He had done everything you can think of. He had walked into the duck pond, and not a stitch of his clothes but had had to be changed. He had climbed on a hay rick and fallen off it, and had not broken his neck, which, as cook told him, he richly deserved to do. He had found a mouse in the trap and put it in the kitchen tea-pot, so that when cook went to make tea it jumped out at her, and affected her to screams followed by tears. Tavy was sorry for this, of course, and said so like a man. He had only, he explained, meant to give her a little start. In the confusion that followed the mouse, he had eaten all the blackcurrant jam that was put out for kitchen tea, and for this too, he apologized handsomely as soon as it was pointed out to him. He had broken a pane of the greenhouse with a stone and . . . But why pursue the painful theme? The last thing he had done was to explore the attic, where he was never allowed to go, and to knock down the White Cat from its shelf.

The sound of its fall brought the servants. The cat was not broken – only its other ear was chipped. Tavy was put to bed. But he got out as soon as the servants had gone downstairs, crept up to the attic, secured the Cat, and washed it in the bath. So that when mother came back from London, Tavy, dancing impatiently at the head of the stairs, in a very wet night-gown, flung himself upon her and cried, 'I've been awfully naughty, and I'm frightfully sorry, and please may I have the White Cat for my very own?'

He was much sorrier than he had expected to be when he saw that mother was too tired even to want to know, as she generally did, exactly how naughty he had been. She only kissed him, and said:

'I am sorry you've been naughty, my darling. Go back to bed now. Good-night.'

Tavy was ashamed to say anything more about the China Cat, so he went back to bed. But he took the Cat with him, and talked to it and kissed it, and went to sleep with its smooth shiny shoulder against his cheek.

In the days that followed, he was extravagantly good. Being good seemed as easy as being bad usually was. This may have been because mother seemed so tired and ill; and gentlemen in black coats and high hats came to see mother, and after they had gone she used to cry. (These things going on in a house sometimes make people good; sometimes they act just the other way.) Or it may have been because he had the China Cat to talk to. Anyhow, whichever way it was, at the end of the week mother said:

'Tavy, you've been a dear good boy, and a great comfort to me. You must have tried very hard to be good.'

It was difficult to say, 'No, I haven't, at least not since the first day,' but Tavy got it said, and was hugged for his pains.

'You wanted', said mother, 'the China Cat. Well, you may have it.'

'For my very own?'

'For your very own. But you must be very careful not to break it. And you mustn't give it away. It goes with the house. Your Aunt Jane made me promise to keep it in the family. It's very, very old. Don't take it out of doors for fear of accidents.'

'I love the White Cat, mother,' said Tavy. 'I love it better'n all my toys.'

Then mother told Tavy several things, and that night when he went to bed Tavy repeated them all faithfully to the China Cat, who was about six inches high and looked very intelligent.

'So you see,' he ended, 'the wicked lawyer's taken nearly all mother's money, and we've got to leave our own lovely big White House, and go and live in a horrid little house with another house glued on to its side. And mother does hate it so.'

'I don't wonder,' said the China Cat very distinctly.

'*What!*' said Tavy, half-way into his night-shirt.

'I said, I don't wonder, Octavius,' said the China Cat, and rose from her sitting position, stretched her china legs and waved her white china tail.

'You can speak?' said Tavy.

'Can't you see I can? – hear I mean?' said the Cat. 'I belong to you now, so I can speak to you. I couldn't before. It wouldn't have been manners.'

Tavy, his night-shirt round his neck, sat down on the edge of the bed with his mouth open.

'Come, don't look so silly,' said the Cat, taking a walk along the high wooden mantelpiece, 'anyone would think you didn't *like* me to talk to you.'

'I *love* you to,' said Tavy recovering himself a little.

'Well then,' said the Cat.

'May I touch you?' Tavy asked timidly.

'Of course! I belong to you. Look out!' The China Cat gathered herself together and jumped. Tavy caught her.

It was quite a shock to find when one stroked her that the China Cat, though alive, was still china, hard, cold, and smooth to the touch, and yet perfectly brisk and absolutely bendable as any flesh and blood cat.

'Dear, dear white pussy,' said Tavy, 'I do love you.'

'And I love you,' purred the Cat, 'otherwise I should never have lowered myself to begin a conversation.'

'I wish you were a real cat,' said Tavy.

'I am,' said the Cat. 'Now how shall we amuse ourselves? I suppose you don't care for sport – mousing, I mean?'

'I never tried,' said Tavy, 'and I think I rather wouldn't.'

'Very well then, Octavius,' said the Cat. 'I'll take you to the White Cat's Castle. Get into bed. Bed makes a good travelling carriage, especially when you haven't any other. Shut your eyes.'

Tavy did as he was told. Shut his eyes, but could not keep them shut. He opened them a tiny, tiny chink, and sprang up. He was not in bed. He was on a couch of soft beast-skin, and the couch stood in a splendid hall, whose walls were of gold and ivory. By him stood the White Cat, no longer china, but real live cat – and fur – as cats should be.

'Here we are,' she said. 'The journey didn't take long, did it? Now we'll have that splendid supper, out of the fairy tale, with the invisible hands waiting on us.'

She clapped her paws – paws now as soft as white velvet – and a table-cloth floated into the room; then knives and forks and spoons and glasses, the table was laid, the dishes drifted in, and they began to eat. There happened to be every single thing Tavy liked best to eat. After supper there was music and singing, and Tavy, having kissed a white, soft, furry forehead, went to bed in a gold four-poster with a counterpane of butterflies' wings. He awoke at home. On the mantelpiece sat the White Cat, looking as though butter would not melt in her mouth. And all her furriness had gone with her voice. She was silent – and china.

Tavy spoke to her. But she would not answer. Nor did she speak all day. Only at night when he was getting into bed she suddenly mewed, stretched, and said:

'Make haste, there's a play acted tonight at my castle.'

Tavy made haste, and was rewarded by another glorious evening in the castle of the White Cat.

And so the weeks went on. Days full of an ordinary little boy's joys and sorrows, goodnesses and badnesses. Nights spent by a little Prince in the Magic Castle of the White Cat.

Then came the day when Tavy's mother spoke to him, and he, very scared and serious, told the China Cat what she had said.

'I knew this would happen,' said the Cat. 'It

always does. So you're to leave your house next week. Well, there's only one way out of the difficulty. Draw your sword, Tavy, and cut off my head and tail.'

'And then will you turn into a Princess, and shall I have to marry you?' Tavy asked with horror.

'No, dear – no,' said the Cat reassuringly. 'I shan't turn into anything. But you and mother will turn into happy people. I shall just not be any more – for you.'

'Then I won't do it,' said Tavy.

'But you must. Come, draw your sword, like a brave fairy Prince, and cut off my head.'

The sword hung above his bed, with the helmet and breast-plate Uncle James had given him last Christmas.

'I'm not a fairy Prince,' said the child. 'I'm Tavy – and I love you.'

'You love your mother better,' said the Cat. 'Come cut my head off. The story always ends like that. You love mother best. It's for her sake.'

'Yes.' Tavy was trying to think it out. 'Yes, I love mother best. But I love *you*. And I won't cut off your head – no, not even for mother.'

'Then,' said the Cat, 'I must do what I can!'

She stood up, waving her white china tail, and before Tavy could stop her she had leapt, not, as before, into his arms, but on to the wide hearthstone.

It was all over – The China Cat lay broken inside the high brass fender. The sound of the smash brought mother running.

'What is it?' she cried. 'Oh, Tavy – the China Cat!'

'She would do it,' sobbed Tavy. 'She wanted me to cut off her head'n I wouldn't.'

'Don't talk nonsense, dear,' said mother sadly. 'That only makes it worse. Pick up the pieces.'

'There's only two pieces,' said Tavy. 'Couldn't you stick her together again?'

'Why,' said mother, holding the pieces close to the candle. 'She's been broken before. And mended.'

'*I* knew that,' said Tavy, still sobbing. 'Oh, my dear White Cat, oh, oh, oh!' The last 'oh' was a howl of anguish.

'Come, crying won't mend her,' said mother. 'Look, there's another piece of her, close to the shovel.'

Tavy stooped.

'That's not a piece of cat,' he said, and picked it up.

It was a pale parchment label, tied to a key. Mother held it to the candle and read: '*Key of the lock behind the knot in the mantelpiece panel in the white parlour.*'

'Tavy! I wonder! But ... where did it come from?'

'Out of my White Cat, I s'pose,' said Tavy, his tears stopping. 'Are you going to see what's in the mantelpiece panel, mother? Are you? Oh, do let me come and see too!'

'You don't deserve,' mother began, and ended, 'Well, put your dressing-gown on then.'

They went down the gallery past the pictures and the stuffed birds and tables with china on them and downstairs on to the white parlour. But they could not see any knot in the mantelpiece panel, because it was all painted white. But mother's fingers felt softly all over it, and found a round raised spot. It was a knot, sure enough. Then she scraped round it with her scissors, till she loosened the knot, and poked it out with the scissors point.

'I don't suppose there's any keyhole there really,' she said. But there was. And what is more, the key fitted. The panel swung open, and inside was a little cupboard with two shelves. What was on the shelves? There were old laces and old embroideries, old jewellery and old silver; there was money, and there were dusty old papers that Tavy thought most uninteresting. But mother did not think them uninteresting. She laughed, and cried, or nearly cried, and said:

'Oh, Tavy, this was why the China Cat was to be taken such care of!' Then she told him how, a hundred and fifty years before, the Head of the House had gone out to fight for the Pretender, and had told his daughter to take the greatest care of the China Cat. 'I will send you word of the reason by a sure hand,' he said, for they parted on the open square, where any spy might have over-heard anything. And he had been killed by an ambush not ten miles from home – and his daugh-ter had never known. But she had kept the Cat.

'And now it has saved us,' said mother. 'We can stay in the dear old house, and there are two other houses that will belong to us too, I think. And, oh, Tavy, would you like some pound-cake and ginger-wine, dear?'

Tavy did like. And had it.

The China Cat was mended, but it was put in the glass-fronted corner cupboard in the drawing-room, because it had saved the house.

Now I dare say you'll think this is all nonsense, and a made-up story. Not at all. If it were, how would you account for Tavy's finding, the very next night, fast asleep on his pillow, his own white Cat – the furry friend that the China Cat used to turn into every evening – the dear hostess who had amused him so well in the White Cat's fairy Palace?

It was she, beyond a doubt, and that was why Tavy didn't mind a bit about the China Cat being taken from him and kept under glass. You may think that it was just any old stray white cat that had come in by accident. Tavy knows better. It has the very same tender tone in its purr that the magic White Cat had. It will not talk to Tavy, it is true; but Tavy can and does talk to it. But the thing that makes it perfectly certain that it is the White Cat is that the tips of its two ears are missing – just as the China Cat's ears were. If you say that it might have lost its ear-tips in battle you are the kind of person who always *makes* difficulties, and you may be quite sure that the kind of splendid magics that happened to Tavy will never happen to *you*.

7

Belinda and Bellamant; or the Bells of Carrillon-land

There is a certain country where a king is never allowed to reign while a queen can be found. They like queens much better than kings in the country. I can't think why. If someone has tried to teach you a little history, you will perhaps think that this is the Salic law. But it isn't. In the biggest city of that odd country there is a great bell-tower (higher than the clock-tower of the Houses of Parliament, where they put MPs who forget their manners). This bell-tower had seven bells in it, very sweet-toned splendid bells, made expressly to ring on the joyful occasions when a princess was born who would be queen some day. And the great tower was built expressly for the bells to ring in. So you see what a lot they thought of queens in that country. Now in all the bells there are Bell-people – it is their voices that you hear when the bells ring. All that about its being the clapper of the bell is mere nonsense, and would hardly deceive a child. I don't know why people say such things. Most Bell-people are very energetic busy folk, who love the sound of their own voices, and hate being idle, and when nearly two hundred years had gone by, and no princesses had been born, they got tired of living in bells that were never rung. So they slipped out of the belfry one fine frosty night, and left the big beautiful bells empty, and went off to find other homes. One of them went to live in a dinner-bell, and one in a school-bell, and the rest all found homes – they did not mind where – just anywhere, in fact, where they could find any Bell-person kind enough to give them board and lodging. And everyone was surprised at the increased loudness in the voices of these hospitable bells. For, of course, the Bell-people from the belfry did their best to help in the housework as polite guests should, and always added their voices to those of their hosts on all occasions when bell-talk was called for. And the seven big beautiful bells in the belfry were left hollow and dark and quite empty, except for the clappers who did not care about the comforts of a home.

Now of course a good house does not remain empty long, especially when there is no rent to pay, and in a very short time the seven bells all had tenants, and they were all the kind of folk that no respectable Bell-people would care to be acquainted with.

They had been turned out of other bells – cracked bells and broken bells, the bells of horses that had been lost in snowstorms or of ships that had gone down at sea. They hated work, and they were a glum, silent, disagreeable people, but as far as they could be pleased about anything they were pleased to live in bells that were never rung, in houses where there was nothing to do. They sat hunched up under the black domes of their houses, dressed in darkness and cobwebs, and their only pleasure was idleness, their only feasts the thick dusty silence that lies heavy in all belfries where the bells never ring. They hardly ever spoke even to each other, and in the whispers that good Bell-people talk in among themselves, and that no one can hear but the bat whose ear for music is very fine and who has himself a particularly high voice, and when they did speak they quarrelled.

And when at last the bells *were* rung for the birth of a Princess the wicked Bell-people were furious. Of course they had to *ring* – a bell can't help that when the rope is pulled – but their voices were so ugly that people were quite shocked.

'What poor taste our ancestors must have had,' they said, 'to think these were good bells!'

(You remember the bells had not rung for nearly two hundred years.)

'Dear me,' said the King to the Queen, 'what odd ideas people had in the old days. I always understood that these bells had beautiful voices.'

'They're quite hideous,' said the Queen. And so they were. Now that night the lazy Bell-folk came down out of the belfry full of anger against the Princess whose birth had disturbed their idleness.

There is no anger like that of a lazy person who is made to work against his will.

And they crept out of the dark domes of their houses and came down in their dust dresses and cobweb cloaks, and crept up to the palace where everyone had gone to bed long before, and stood round the mother-of-pearl cradle where the baby princess lay asleep. And they reached their seven dark right hands out across the white satin coverlet, and the oldest and hoarsest and laziest said:

'She shall grow uglier every day, except Sundays, and every Sunday she shall be seven times prettier than the Sunday before.'

'Why not uglier every day, and a double dose on Sunday?' asked the youngest and spitefullest of the wicked Bell-people.

'Because there's no rule without an exception,' said the eldest and hoarsest and laziest, 'and she'll feel it all the more if she's pretty once a week. And,' he added, 'this shall go on till she finds a bell that doesn't ring, and can't ring, and never will ring, and wasn't made to ring.'

'Why not for ever?' asked the young and spiteful.

'Nothing goes on for ever,' said the eldest Bell-person, 'not even ill-luck. And we have to leave her a way out. It doesn't matter. She'll never know what it is. Let alone finding it.'

Then they went back to the belfry and rearranged as well as they could the comfortable web-and-owls'-nest furniture of their houses which had all been shaken up and disarranged by that absurd ringing of bells at the birth of a Princess that nobody could really be pleased about.

When the Princess was two weeks old the King said to the Queen:

'My love – the Princess is not so handsome as I thought she was.'

'Nonsense, Henry,' said the Queen, 'the light's not good, that's all.'

Next day – it was Sunday – the King pulled back the lace curtains of the cradle and said:

'The light's good enough now – and you see she's –'

He stopped.

'It *must* have been the light,' he said, 'she looks all right to-day.'

'Of course she does, a precious,' said the Queen.

But on Monday morning His Majesty was quite sure really that the Princess was rather plain, for a Princess. And when Sunday came, and the Princess had on her best robe and the cap with the little white ribbons in the frill, he rubbed his nose and said there was no doubt dress did make a great deal of difference. For the Princess was now as pretty as a new daisy.

The Princess was several years old before her mother could be got to see that it really was better for the child to wear plain clothes and a veil on weekdays. On Sundays, of course she could wear her best frock and a clean crown just like anybody else.

Of course nobody ever told the Princess how ugly she was. She wore a veil on weekdays, and so did everyone else in the palace, and she was never allowed to look in the glass except on Sundays, so that she had no idea that she was not as pretty all the week as she was on the first day of it. She grew up therefore quite contented. But the parents were in despair.

'Because,' said King Henry, 'it's high time she was married. We ought to choose a king to rule the realm – I have always looked forward to her marrying at twenty-one – and to our retiring on a modest competence to some nice little place in the country where we could have a few pigs.'

'And a cow,' said the Queen, wiping her eyes.

'And a pony and trap,' said the King.

'And hens,' said the Queen, 'yes. And now it can never, never be. Look at the child! I just ask you! Look at her!'

'*No,*' said the King firmly, 'I haven't done that since she was ten, except on Sundays.'

'Couldn't we get a prince to agree to a "Sunday only" marriage – not let him see her during the week?'

'Such an unusual arrangement', said the King, 'would involve very awkward explanations, and I can't think of any except the true ones, which would be quite impossible to give. You see, we should want a first-class prince, and no really high-toned Highness would take a wife on those terms.'

'It's a thoroughly comfortable kingdom,' said the Queen doubtfully. 'The young man would be handsomely provided for for life.'

'I couldn't marry Belinda to a time-server or a place-worshipper,' said the King decidedly.

Meanwhile the Princess had taken the matter into her own hands. She had fallen in love.

You know, of course, that a handsome book is sent out every year to all the kings who have daughters to marry. It is rather like the illustrated catalogues of Liberty's or Peter Robinson's, only instead of illustrations showing furniture or ladies' cloaks and dresses, the pictures are all of princes who are of an age to be married, and are looking out for suitable wives. The book is called the *Royal Match Catalogue Illustrated,* – and besides the pictures of the princes it has little printed bits about their incomes, accomplishments, prospects, and tempers, and relations.

Now the Princess saw this book – which is never shown to princesses, but only to their parents – it was carelessly left lying on the round table in the parlour. She looked all through it, and she hated each prince more than the one before till she came to the very end, and on the last page of all, screwed away in a corner, was the picture of a prince who was quite as good-looking as a prince has any call to be.

'I like *you,*' said Belinda softly. Then she read the little bit of print underneath.

Prince Bellamant, aged twenty-four. Wants Prin-

cess who doesn't object to a christening curse. Nature of curse only revealed in the strictest confidence. Good tempered. Comfortably off. Quiet habits. No relations.

'Poor dear,' said the Princess. 'I wonder what the curse is! I'm sure *I* shouldn't mind!'

The blue dusk of evening was deepening in the garden outside. The Princess rang for the lamp and went to draw the curtain. There was a rustle and a faint high squeak – and something black flopped on to the floor and fluttered there.

'Oh – it's a bat,' cried the Princess, as the lamp came in. 'I don't like bats.'

'Let me fetch a dust-pan and brush and sweep the nasty thing away,' said the parlourmaid.

'No, no,' said Belinda, 'it's hurt, poor dear,' and though she hated bats she picked it up. It was horribly cold to touch, one wing dragged loosely. 'You can go, Jane,' said the Princess to the parlourmaid.

Then she got a big velvet-covered box that had had chocolate in it, and put some cotton wool in it and said to the Bat:

'You poor dear, is that comfortable?' and the Bat said:

'Quite, thanks.'

'Good gracious,' said the Princess jumping. 'I didn't know bats could talk.'

'Everyone can talk,' said the Bat, 'but not everyone can hear other people talking. You have a fine ear as well as a fine heart.'

'Will your wing ever get well?' asked the Princess.

'I hope so,' said the Bat. 'But let's talk about you. Do you know why you wear a veil every day except Sundays?'

'Doesn't everybody?' asked Belinda.

'Only here in the palace,' said the Bat, 'that's on your account.'

'But why?' asked the Princess.

'Look in the glass and you'll know.'

'But it's wicked to look in the glass except on Sundays – and besides they're all put away,' said the Princess.

'If I were you,' said the Bat, 'I should go up into the attic where the youngest kitchenmaid sleeps. Feel between the thatch and the wall just above her pillow, and you'll find a little round looking-glass. But come back here before you look at it.'

The Princess did exactly what the Bat told her to do, and when she had come back into the parlour and shut the door she looked in the little round glass that the youngest kitchenmaid's sweetheart had given her. And when she saw her ugly, ugly, ugly face – for you must remember she had been growing uglier every day since she was born – she screamed and then she said:

'That's not me, it's a horrid picture.'

'It *is* you, though,' said the Bat firmly but kindly; 'and now you see why you wear a veil all the week – and only look in the glass on Sunday.'

'But why,' asked the Princess in tears, 'why don't I look like that in the Sunday looking-glasses?'

'Because you aren't like that on Sundays,' the Bat replied. 'Come,' it went on, 'stop crying. I didn't tell you the dread secret of your ugliness just to make you cry – but because I know the way for you to be as pretty all the week as you are on Sundays, and since you've been so kind to me I'll tell you. Sit down close beside me, it fatigues me to speak loud.'

The Princess did, and listened through her veil and her tears, while the Bat told her all that I began this story by telling you.

'My great-great-great-great-grandfather heard the tale years ago,' he said, 'up in the dark, dusty, beautiful, comfortable, cobwebby belfry, and I have heard scraps of it myself when the evil Bell-people were quarrelling, or talking in their sleep, lazy things!'

'It's very good of you to tell me all this,' said Belinda, 'but what am I to do?'

'You must find the bell that doesn't ring, and can't ring, and never will ring, and wasn't made to ring.'

'If I were a prince,' said the Princess, 'I could go out and seek my fortune.'

'Princesses have fortunes as well as princes,' said the Bat.

'But father and mother would never let me go and look for mine.'

'Think!' said the Bat, 'perhaps you'll find a way.'

So Belinda thought and thought. And at last she got the book that had the portraits of eligible princes in it, and she wrote to the prince who had the christening curse – and this is what she said:

'Princess Belinda of Carrillon-land is not afraid of christening curses. If Prince Bellamant would like to marry her he had better apply to her Royal Father in the usual way.

'*PS* – I have seen your portrait.'

When the Prince got this letter he was very pleased, and wrote at once for Princess Belinda's likeness. Of course they sent him a picture of her Sunday face, which was the most beautiful face in the world. As soon as he saw it he knew that this was not only the most beautiful face in the world, but the dearest, so he wrote to her father by the next post – applying for her hand in the usual way and enclosing the most respectable references. The King told the Princess:

'Come,' said he, 'what do you say to this young man?'

And the Princess, of course, said, 'Yes, please.'

So the wedding-day was fixed for the first Sunday in June.

But when the Prince arrived with all his glorious following of courtiers and men-at-arms, with two pink peacocks and a crown-case full of diamonds for his bride, he absolutely refused to be married on a Sunday. Nor would he give any reason for his refusal. And then the King lost his temper and broke off the match, and the Prince went away.

But he did not go very far. That night he bribed a page-boy to show him which was the Princess's room, and he climbed up by the jasmine through the dark rose-scented night, and tapped at the window.

'Who's dhere?' said the Princess inside in the dark.

'Me,' said the Prince in the dark outside.

'Thed id wasnd't true?' said the Princess. 'They toad be you'd ridded away.'

'What a cold you've got, my Princess,' said the Prince hanging on by the jasmine boughs.

'It's not a cold,' sniffed the Princess.

'Then . . . oh you dear . . . were you crying because you thought I'd gone?' he said.

'I suppose so,' said she.

He said, 'You dear!' again, and kissed her hands.

'*Why* wouldn't you be married on a Sunday?' she asked.

'It's the curse, dearest,' he explained, 'I couldn't tell anyone but you. The fact is Malevola wasn't asked to my christening so she doomed me to be . . . well, she said "moderately good-looking all the week, and too ugly for words on Sundays". So you see! You *will* be married on a weekday, won't you?'

'But I can't,' said the Princess, 'because I've

got a curse too – only I'm ugly all the week and pretty on Sundays.'

'How extremely tiresome,' said the Prince, 'but can't you be cured?'

'Oh yes,' said the Princess, and told him how. 'And you,' she asked, 'is yours quite incurable?'

'Not at all,' he answered, 'I've only got to stay under water for five minutes and the spell will be broken. But you see, beloved, the difficulty is that I can't do it. I've practised regularly, from a boy, in the sea, and in the swimming bath, and even in my wash-hand basin – hours at a time I've practised – but I never can keep under more than two minutes.'

'Oh dear,' said the Princess, 'this is dreadful.'

'It is rather trying,' the Prince answered.

'You're sure you like me,' she asked suddenly, 'now you know that I'm only pretty once a week?'

'I'd die for you,' said he.

'Then I'll tell you what. Send all your courtiers away, and take a situation as under-gardener here – I know we want one. And then every night I'll climb down the jasmine and we'll go out together and seek our fortune. I'm sure we shall find it.'

And they did go out. The very next night, and the next, and the next, and the next, and the next, and the next. And they did not find their fortunes, but they got fonder and fonder of each other. They could not see each other's faces, but they held hands as they went along through the dark.

And on the seventh night, as they passed by a

house that showed chinks of light through its
shutters, they heard a bell being rung outside for
supper, a bell with a very loud and beautiful
voice. But instead of saying: 'Supper's ready,'
as anyone would have expected, the bell was
saying:

> Ding dong dell!
> *I* could tell
> Where you ought to go
> To break the spell.

Then someone left off ringing the bell, so of
course it couldn't say any more. So the two went on.
A little way down the road a cow-bell tinkled behind the wet hedge of the lane. And it said – not,
'Here I am, quite safe,' as a cow-bell should, but:

> Ding dong dell
> All will be well
> If you . . .

Then the cow stopped walking and began to
eat, so the bell couldn't say any more. The Prince
and Princess went on, and you will not be surprised to hear that they heard the voices of five
more bells that night. The next was a school-bell.
The schoolmaster's little boy thought it would be
fun to ring it very late at night – but his father
came and caught him before the bell could say
any more than:

> Ding a dong dell
> You can break up the spell
> By taking . . .

So that was no good.

Then there were the three bells that were the sign over the door of an inn where people were happily dancing to a fiddle, because there was a wedding. These bells said:

> We are the
> Merry three
> Bells, bells, bells.
> You are two
> To undo
> Spells, spells, spells . . .

Then the wind who was swinging the bells suddenly thought of an appointment he had made with a pine forest, to get up an entertaining imitation of sea-waves for the benefit of the forest nymphs who had never been to the seaside, and he went off – so, of course, the bells couldn't ring any more, and the Prince and Princess went on down the dark road.

There was a cottage and the Princess pulled her veil closely over her face, for yellow light streamed from its open door – and it was a Wednesday.

Inside a little boy was sitting on the floor – quite a little boy – he ought to have been in bed long before, and I don't know why he wasn't. And he was ringing a little tinkling bell that had dropped off a sleigh.

And this little bell said:

Tinkle, tinkle, tinkle, I'm a little sleigh-bell,
But I know what I know, and I'll tell, tell, tell.
Find the Enchanter of the Ringing Well,
He will show you how to break the spell, spell,
   spell.
Tinkle, tinkle, tinkle, I'm a little sleigh-bell,
But I know what I know . . .

And so on, over and over, again and again, because the little boy was quite contented to go on shaking his sleigh-bell for ever and ever.

'So now we know,' said the Prince, 'isn't that glorious?'

'Yes, very, but where's the Enchanter of the Ringing Well?' said the Princess doubtfully.

'Oh, I've got *his* address in my pocket-book,' said the Prince. 'He's my god-father. He was one of the references I gave your father.'

So the next night the Prince brought a horse to the garden, and he and the Princess mounted, and rode, and rode, and rode, and in the grey dawn they came to Wonderwood, and in the very middle of that the Magician's Palace stands.

The Princess did not like to call on a perfect stranger so very early in the morning, so they decided to wait a little and look about them.

The castle was very beautiful, decorated with a conventional design of bells and bell ropes, carved in white stone.

Luxuriant plants of American bell-vine covered the drawbridge and portcullis. On a green lawn in front of the castle was a well, with a curious bell-shaped covering suspended over it. The lovers leaned over the mossy fern-grown wall of the well, and, looking down, they could see that the narrowness of the well only lasted for a few feet, and below that it spread into a cavern where water lay in a big pool.

'What cheer?' said a pleasant voice behind them. It was the Enchanter, an early riser, like Darwin was, and all other great scientific men.

They told him what cheer.

'But,' Prince Bellamant ended, 'it's really no use. I can't keep under water more than two minutes however much I try. And my precious Belinda's not likely to find any silly old bell that doesn't ring, and can't ring, and never will ring, and was never made to ring.'

'Ho, ho,' laughed the Enchanter with the soft full laughter of old age. 'You've come to the right shop. Who told you?'

'The bells,' said Belinda.

'Ah, yes.' The old man frowned kindly upon them. 'You must be very fond of each other?'

'We are,' said the two together.

'Yes,' the Enchanter answered, 'because only true lovers can hear the true speech of the bells, and then only when they're together. Well, there's the bell!'

He pointed to the covering of the well, went forward, and touched some lever or spring. The covering swung out from above the well, and hung over the grass grey with the dew of dawn.

'*That?*' said Bellamant.

'That,' said his god-father. 'It doesn't ring, and it can't ring, and it never will ring, and it was never made to ring. Get into it.'

'Eh?' said Bellamant forgetting his manners.

The old man took a hand of each and led them under the bell.

They looked up. It had windows of thick glass, and high seats about four feet from its edge, running all round inside.

'Take your seats,' said the Enchanter.

Bellamant lifted his Princess to the bench and leaped up beside her.

'Now,' said the old man, 'sit still, hold each other's hands and for your lives don't move.'

He went away, and next moment they felt the bell swing in the air. It swung round till once more it was over the well, and then it went down, down, down.

'I'm not afraid with you,' said Belinda, because she was, dreadfully.

Down went the bell. The glass windows leaped into light, looking through them the two could see blurred glories of lamps in the side of the cave, magic lamps, or perhaps merely electric, which, curiously enough, have ceased to seem magic to us nowadays. Then with a plop the lower edge of the bell met the water, the water rose inside it, a little, then not any more. And the bell went down, down, and above their heads the green water lapped against the windows of the bell.

'You're under water – if we stay five minutes,' Belinda whispered.

'Yes, dear,' said Bellamant, and pulled out his ruby-studded chronometer.

'It's five minutes for you, but oh!' cried Belinda, 'it's *now* for me. For I've found the bell that doesn't ring, and can't ring, and never will ring, and wasn't made to ring. Oh Bellamant dearest, it's Thursday. *Have* I got my Sunday face?'

She tore away her veil, and his eyes, fixed upon her face, could not leave it.

'Oh dream of all the world's delight,' he murmured, 'how beautiful you are.'

Neither spoke again till a sudden little shock told them that the bell was moving up again.

'Nonsense,' said Bellamant, 'it's not five minutes.'

But when they looked at the ruby-studded chronometer, it was nearly three-quarters of an hour. But then, of course, the well was enchanted!

'Magic? Nonsense,' said the old man when they hung about him with thanks and pretty words. 'It's only a diving-bell. My own invention.'

★

So they went home and were married, and the Princess did not wear a veil at the wedding. She said she had had enough veils to last her time.

And a year and a day after that a little daughter was born to them.

'Now sweetheart,' said King Bellamant – he was king now because the old king and queen had retired from the business, and were keeping pigs and hens in the country as they had always planned to do – 'dear sweetheart and life's love, I am going to ring the bells with my own hands, to show how glad I am for you, and for the child, and for our good life together.'

So he went out. It was very dark, because the baby princess had chosen to be born at midnight.

The King went out to the belfry, that stood in the great, bare, quiet, moonlit square, and he opened the door. The furry-pussy bell-ropes, like huge caterpillars, hung on the first loft. The King began to climb the curly-wurly stone stair. And as he went up he heard a noise, the strangest noises, stamping and rustling and deep breathings.

He stood still in the ringers' loft where the pussy-furry caterpillary bell-ropes hung, and from the belfry above he heard the noise of strong fighting, and mixed with it the sound of voices angry and desperate, but with a noble note that thrilled the soul of the hearer like the sound of the trumpet in battle. And the voices cried:

> Down, down – away, away,
> When good has come ill may not stay,
> Out, out, into the night,
> The belfry bells are ours by right!

And the words broke and joined again, like water when it flows against the piers of a bridge. 'Down, down . . . Ill may not stay . . .' 'Good has come . . .' 'Away, away . . .' And the joining came like the sound of the river that flows free again.

> Out, out, into the night,
> The belfry bells are ours by right!

And then, as King Bellamant stood there, thrilled and yet, as it were, turned to stone, by the magic of this conflict that raged above him, there came a sweeping rush down the belfry ladder. The lantern he carried showed him a rout of little, dark, evil people, clothed in dust and cobwebs, that scurried down the wooden steps gnashing their teeth and growling in the bitterness of a deserved defeat. They passed and there was silence. Then the King flew from rope to rope pulling lustily, and from above, the bells answered in their own clear beautiful voices – because the good Bell-folk had driven out the usurpers and had come to their own again:

Ring-a-ring-a-ring-a-ring-a-ring! Ring, bell!
A little baby comes on earth to dwell. Ring, bell!

Sound bell! Sound! Swell!
Ring for joy and wish her well!
May her life tell
No tale of ill-spell!
Ring, bell! Joy, bell! Love, bell!
Ring!

'But I don't see,' said King Bellamant, when he had told Queen Belinda all about it, 'how it was that I came to hear them. The Enchanter of the Ringing Well said that only lovers could hear what the bells had to say, and then only when they were together.'

'You silly dear boy,' said Queen Belinda, cuddling the baby princess close under her chin, 'we *are* lovers, aren't we? And you don't suppose I wasn't with you when you went to ring the bells for our baby – my heart and soul anyway – all of me that matters!'

'Yes,' said the King, 'of course you were. That accounts!'

'Auntie! No, no, no! I will be good. Oh, I will!'
The little weak voice came from the other side of
the locked attic door.

'You should have thought of that before,' said
the strong, sharp voice outside.

'I didn't mean to be naughty. I didn't, truly.'

'It's not what you mean, miss, it's what you do.
I'll teach you not to mean, my lady.'

The bitter irony of the last words dried the
child's tears. 'Very well, then,' she screamed, 'I
won't be good; I won't try to be good. I thought
you'd like your nasty old garden weeded. I only
did it to please you. How was I to know it was
turnips? It looked just like weeds.' Then came a
pause, then another shriek. 'Oh, Auntie, don't!
Oh, let me out – let me out!'

'I'll not let you out till I've broken your spirit,
my girl; you may rely on that.'

The sharp voice stopped abruptly on a high
note; determined feet in strong boots sounded on
the stairs – fainter, fainter; a door slammed below
with a dreadful definiteness, and Elsie was left
alone, to wonder how soon her spirit would break

– for at no less a price, it appeared, could freedom be bought.

The outlook seemed hopeless. The martyrs and heroines, with whom Elsie usually identified herself, *their* spirit had never been broken; not chains nor the rack nor the fiery stake itself had even weakened them. Imprisonment in an attic would to them have been luxury compared with the boiling oil and the smoking faggots and all the intimate cruelties of mysterious instruments of steel and leather, in cold dungeons, lit only by the dull flare of torches and the bright, watchful eyes of inquisitors.

A month in the house of 'Auntie' self-styled, and really only an unrelated Mrs Staines, paid to take care of the child, had held but one interest – *Foxe's Book of Martyrs*. It was a horrible book – the thick oleographs, their guarding sheets of tissue paper sticking to the prints like bandages to a wound . . . Elsie knew all about wounds: she had had one herself. Only a scalded hand, it is true, but a wound is a wound, all the world over. It was a book that made you afraid to go to bed; but it was a book you could not help reading. And now it seemed as though it might at last help, and not merely sicken and terrify. But the help was frail, and broke almost instantly on the thought – '*They* were brave because they were good: how can I be brave when there's nothing to be brave about except me not knowing the difference between turnips and weeds?'

She sank down, a huddled black bunch on the bare attic floor, and called wildly to someone who could not answer her. Her frock was black because the one who always used to answer could not answer any more. And her father was in India, where you cannot answer, or even hear, your little girl, however much she cries in England.

'I won't cry,' said Elsie, sobbing as violently as ever. 'I can be brave, even if I'm not a saint but only a turnip-mistaker. I'll be a Bastille prisoner, and tame a mouse!' She dried her eyes, though the bosom of the black frock still heaved like the sea after a storm, and looked about for a mouse to tame. One could not begin too soon. But unfortunately there seemed to be no mouse at liberty just then. There were mouse-holes right enough, all round the wainscot, and in the broad, time-worn boards of the old floor. But never a mouse.

'Mouse, mouse!' Elsie called softly. 'Mousie, mousie, come and be tamed!'

Not a mouse replied.

The attic was perfectly empty and dreadfully clean. The other attic, Elsie knew, had lots of interesting things in it – old furniture and saddles, and sacks of seed potatoes – but in this attic nothing. Not so much as a bit of string on the floor that one could make knots in, or twist round one's finger till it made the red ridges that are so interesting to look at afterwards; not even a piece of paper in the draughty, cold fireplace that one could make paper boats of, or prick letters in with a pin or the tag of one's shoe-laces.

As she stooped to see whether under the grate some old match-box or bit of twig might have escaped the broom, she saw suddenly what she had wanted most – a mouse. It was lying on its side. She put out her hand very slowly and gently, and whispered in her softest tones, 'Wake up, Mousie, wake up, and come and be tamed.' But the mouse never moved. And when she took it in her hand it was cold.

'Oh,' she moaned, 'you're dead, and now I can never tame you,' and she sat on the cold hearth and cried again, with the dead mouse in her lap.

'Don't cry,' said somebody. 'I'll find you something to tame – if you really want it.'

Elsie started and saw the head of a black bird peering at her through the square opening that leads to the chimney. The edges of him looked ragged and rainbow-coloured, but that was because she saw him through tears. To a tearless eye he was black and very smooth and sleek.

'Oh!' she said, and nothing more.

'Quite so,' said the bird politely. 'You are surprised to hear me speak, but your surprise will be, of course, much less when I tell you that I am really a Prime Minister condemned by an Enchanter to wear the form of a crow till . . . till I can get rid of it.'

'Oh!' said Elsie.

'Yes, indeed,' said the Crow, and suddenly grew smaller till he could come comfortably through the square opening. He did this, perched on the top bar, and hopped to the floor. And there he got bigger and bigger, and bigger and bigger and bigger. Elsie had scrambled to her feet, and then a black little girl of eight and of the usual size stood face to face with a crow as big as a man, and no doubt as old. She found words then.

'Oh, don't!' she cried. 'Don't get any bigger. I can't bear it.'

'*I* can't *do* it,' said the Crow kindly, 'so that's all right. I thought you'd better get used to seeing rather large crows before I take you to Crownowland. We are all life-size there.'

'But a crow's life-size isn't a man's life-size,' Elsie managed to say.

'Oh yes, it is – when it's an enchanted Crow,' the bird replied. 'That makes all the difference. Now you were saying you wanted to tame something. If you'll come with me to Crownowland I'll show you something worth taming.'

'Is Crow-what's-its-name a nice place?' Elsie asked cautiously. She was, somehow, not so very frightened now.

'Very,' said the Crow.

'Then perhaps I shall like it so much I shan't want to be taming things.'

'Oh yes, you will, when you know how much depends on it.'

'But I shouldn't like', said Elsie, 'to go up the chimney. This isn't my best frock, of course, but still . . .'

'Quite so,' said the Crow. 'I only came that way for fun, and because I can fly. You shall go in by the chief gate of the kingdom, like a lady. Do come.'

But Elsie still hesitated. 'What sort of thing is it you want me to tame?' she said doubtfully.

The enormous crow hesitated. 'A – a sort of lizard,' it said at last. 'And if you can only tame it so that it will do what you tell it to, you'll save the whole kingdom, and we'll put up a statue to you; but not in the People's Park, unless they wish it,' the bird added mysteriously.

'I should like to save a kingdom,' said Elsie, 'and I like lizards. I've seen lots of them in India.'

'Then you'll come?' said the Crow.

'Yes. But how do we go?'

'There are only two doors out of this world into another,' said the Crow. 'I'll take you through the nearest. Allow me!' It puts its wing round her so that her face nestled against the black softness of the under-wing feathers. It was warm and dark and sleepy there, and very comfortable. For a moment she seemed to swim easily in a soft sea of dreams. Then, with a little shock, she found herself standing on a marble terrace, looking out over a city far more beautiful and wonderful than she had ever seen or imagined. The great man-sized Crow was by her side.

'Now,' it said, pointing with the longest of its long black wing-feathers, 'you see this beautiful city?'

'Yes,' said Elsie, 'of course I do.'

'Well . . . I hardly like to tell you the story,' said the Crow, 'but it's a long time ago, and I hope you won't think the worse of us – because we're really very sorry.'

'If you're really sorry,' said Elsie primly, 'of course it's all right.'

'Unfortunately it isn't,' said the Crow. 'You see the great square down there?'

Elsie looked down on a square of green trees, broken a little towards the middle.

'Well, that's where the . . . where *it* is – what you've got to tame, you know.'

'But what did you do that was wrong?'

'We were unkind,' said the Crow slowly, 'and unjust, and ungenerous. We had servants and workpeople doing everything for us; we had nothing to do *but* be kind. And we weren't.'

'Dear me,' said Elsie feebly.

'We had several warnings,' said the Crow. 'There was an old parchment, and it said just how you ought to behave and all that. But we didn't care what it said. I was Court Magician as well as Prime Minister, and I ought to have known better, but I didn't. We all wore frock-coats and high hats then,' he added sadly.

'Go on,' said Elsie, her eyes wandering from one beautiful building to another of the many that nestled among the trees of the city.

'And the old parchment said that if we didn't behave well our bodies would grow like our souls.

But we didn't think so. And then all in a minute they *did* – and we were crows, and our bodies were as black as our souls. Our souls are quite white now,' it added reassuringly.

'But what was *the* dreadful thing you'd done?'

'We'd been unkind to the people who worked for us – not given them enough food or clothes or fire, and at last we took away even their play. There was a big park that the people played in, and we built a wall round it and took it for ourselves, and the King was going to set a statue of himself up in the middle. And then before we could begin to enjoy it we were turned into big black crows; and the working people into big white pigeons – and *they* can go where they like, but we have to stay here till we've tamed the . . . We never can go into the park, until we've settled the thing that guards it. And that thing's a big, big lizard – in fact . . . it's a *dragon!*'

'*Oh!*' cried Elsie; but she was not as frightened as the Crow seemed to expect. Because every now and then she had felt sure that she was really safe in her own bed, and that this was a dream. It was not a dream, but the belief that it was made her very brave, and she felt quite sure that she could settle a dragon, if necessary – a dream dragon, that is. And the rest of the time she thought about *Foxe's Book of Martyrs* and what a heroine she now had the chance to be.

'You want me to kill it?' she asked.

'Oh no! To tame it,' said the Crow. 'We've tried

all sorts of means – long whips, like people tame horses with, and red-hot bars, such as lion-tamers use – and it's all been perfectly useless; and there the dragon lives, and will live till someone can tame him and get him to follow them like a tame fawn, and eat out of their hand.'

'What does the dragon *like* to eat?' Elsie asked.

'*Crows*,' replied the other in an uncomfortable whisper. 'At least *I've* never known it eat anything else!'

'Am I to try to tame it *now*?' Elsie asked.

'Oh dear no,' said the Crow. 'We'll have a banquet in your honour, and you shall have tea with the Princess.'

'How do you know who is a princess and who's not, if you're all crows?' Elsie cried.

'How do you know one human being from another?' the Crow replied. 'Besides . . . Come on to the Palace.'

It led her along the terrace, and down some marble steps to a small arched door. 'The tradesmen's entrance,' it explained. 'Excuse it – the courtiers are crowding in by the front door.' Then through long corridors and passages they went, and at last into the throne-room. Many crows stood about in respectful attitudes. On the golden throne, leaning a gloomy head upon the first joint of his right wing, the Sovereign of Crownowland was musing dejectedly. A little girl of about Elsie's age sat on the steps of the throne nursing a handsome doll.

'Who is the little girl?' Elsie asked.

'*Curtsey!* That's the Princess,' the Prime Minister Crow whispered; and Elsie made the best curtsey she could think of in such a hurry. 'She wasn't wicked enough to be turned into a crow, or poor enough to be turned into a pigeon, so she remains a dear little girl, just as she always was.'

The Princess dropped her doll and ran down the steps of the throne to meet Elsie.

'You dear!' she said. 'You've come to play with me, haven't you? All the little girls I used to play with have turned into crows, and their beaks are *so* awkward at doll's tea-parties, and wings are no good to nurse dollies with. Let's have a doll's tea-party *now*, shall we?'

'May we?' Elsie looked at the Crow King, who nodded his head hopelessly. So, hand in hand, they went.

I wonder whether you have ever had the run of a perfectly beautiful palace and a nursery absolutely crammed with all the toys you ever had or wanted to have: dolls' houses, dolls' china tea-sets, rocking-horses, bricks, nine-pins, paint-boxes, conjuring tricks, pewter dinner-services, and any number of dolls – all most agreeable and distinguished. If you have, you may perhaps be able faintly to imagine Elsie's happiness. And better than all the toys was the Princess Perdona – so gentle and kind and jolly, full of ideas for games, and surrounded by the means for playing them. Think of it, after that bare attic, with not even a bit of string to play with, and no company but the poor little dead mouse!

There is no room in this story to tell you of all the games they had. I can only say that the time went by so quickly that they never noticed it going, and were amazed when the Crow nurse-maid brought in the royal tea-tray. Tea was a beautiful meal – with pink iced cake in it.

Now, all the time that these glorious games had been going on, and this magnificent tea, the wisest crows of Crownowland had been holding a council. They had decided that there was no time like the present, and that Elsie had better try to tame the dragon soon as late. 'But,' the King said, 'she mustn't run any risks. A guard of fifty stalwart crows must go with her, and if the dragon shows the least temper, fifty crows must throw themselves between her and danger, even if it cost fifty-one crow-lives. For I myself will lead that band. Who will volunteer?'

Volunteers, to the number of some thousands, instantly stepped forward, and the Field Marshal selected fifty of the strongest crows.

And then, in the pleasant pinkness of the sunset, Elsie was led out on to the palace steps, where the King made a speech and said what a heroine she was, and how like Joan of Arc. And the crows, who had gathered from all parts of the town cheered madly. Did you ever hear crows cheering? It is a wonderful sound.

Then Elsie got into a magnificent gilt coach,

drawn by eight white horses, with a crow at the head of each horse. The Princess sat with her on the blue velvet cushions and held her hand.

'I *know* you'll do it,' said she; 'you're so brave and clever, Elsie!'

And Elsie felt braver than before, although now it did not seem so like a dream. But she thought of the martyrs, and held Perdona's hand very tight.

At the gates of the green park the Princess kissed and hugged her new friend – her state crown, which she had put on in honour of the occasion, got pushed quite on one side in the warmth of her embrace – and Elsie stepped out of the carriage. There was a great crowd of crows round the park gates, and every one cheered and shouted, 'Speech, speech!'

Elsie got as far as 'Ladies and gentlemen – Crows, I mean,' and then she could not think of anything more, so she simply added, 'Please, I'm ready.'

I wish you could have heard those crows cheer.

But Elsie wouldn't have the escort.

'It's very kind,' she said, 'but the dragon only eats crows, and I'm not a crow, thank goodness – I mean I'm not a crow – and if I've got to be brave I'd like to *be* brave, and none of you to get eaten. If only someone will come with me to show me the way and then run back as hard as he can when we get near the dragon. *Please!*'

'If only one goes *I* shall be the one,' said the

King. And he and Elsie went through the great
gates side by side. She held the end of his wing,
which was the nearest they could get to hand in
hand.

The crowd outside waited in breathless silence.
Elsie and the King went on through the winding
paths of the People's Park. And by the winding
paths they came at last to the Dragon. He lay very
peacefully on a great stone slab, his enormous
bat-like wings spread out on the grass and his
goldy-green scales glittering in the pretty pink
sunset light.

'Go back!' said Elsie.

'No,' said the King.

'If you don't,' said Elsie, '*I* won't go *on*. Seeing
a crow might rouse him to fury, or give him an
appetite, or something. Do – do go!'

So he went, but not far. He hid behind a tree,
and from its shelter he watched.

Elsie drew a long breath. Her heart was thump-
ing under the black frock. 'Suppose,' she thought,
'he takes me for a crow!' But she thought how
yellow her hair was, and decided that the dragon
would be certain to notice that.

'Quick march!' she said to herself, 'remember
Joan of Arc,' and walked right up to the dragon.
It never moved, but watched her suspiciously out
of its bright green eyes.

'Dragon dear!' she said in her clear little voice.

'*Eh?*' said the dragon, in tones of extreme
astonishment.

'Dragon dear,' she repeated, 'do you like sugar?'

'*Yes*,' said the dragon.

'Well, I've brought you some. You won't hurt me if I bring it to you?'

The dragon violently shook its vast head.

'It's not much,' said Elsie, 'but I saved it at tea-time. Four lumps. Two for each of my mugs of milk.'

She laid the sugar on the stone slab by the dragon's paw.

It turned its head towards the sugar. The pinky sunset light fell on its face, and Elsie saw that it was weeping! Great fat tears as big as prize pears were coursing down its wrinkled cheeks.

'Oh, don't,' said Elsie, '*don't* cry! Poor dragon, what's the matter?'

'Oh!' sobbed the dragon, 'I'm only so glad you've come. I – I've been so lonely. No one to love me. You *do* love me, don't you?'

'I – I'm sure I shall when I know you better,' said Elsie kindly.

'Give me a kiss, dear,' said the dragon, sniffing.

It is no joke to kiss a dragon. But Elsie did it – somewhere on the hard green wrinkles of its forehead.

'Oh, *thank* you,' said the dragon, brushing away its tears with the tip of its tail. 'That breaks the charm. I can move now. And I've got back all my lost wisdom. Come along – I *do* want my tea!'

So, to the waiting crowd at the gate came Elsie

and the dragon side by side. And at sight of the dragon, tamed, a great shout went up from the crowd; and at that shout each one in the crowd turned quickly to the next one – for it was the shout of men, and not of crows. Because at the first sight of the dragon, tamed, they had left off being crows for ever and ever, and once again were men.

The King came running through the gates, his royal robes held high, so that he shouldn't trip over them, and he too was no longer a crow, but a man.

And what did Elsie feel after being so brave? Well, she felt that she would like to cry, and also to laugh, and she felt that she loved not only the dragon, but every man, woman, and child in the whole world – even Mrs Staines.

She rode back to the Palace on the dragon's back.

And as they went the crowd of citizens who had been crows met the crowd of citizens who had been pigeons, and these were poor men in poor clothes.

It would have done you good to see how the ones who had been rich and crows ran to meet the ones who had been pigeons and poor.

'Come and stay at my house, brother,' they cried to those who had no homes. 'Brother, I have many coats, come and choose some,' they cried to the ragged. 'Come and feast with me!' they cried to all. And the rich and the poor went off arm in arm to feast and be glad that night, and the next day to work side by side. 'For,' said the King, speaking with his hand on the neck of the tamed dragon, 'our land has been called Crownowland. But we are no longer crows. We are men: and we will be Just men. And our country shall be called Justnowland for ever and ever. And for the future we shall not be rich and poor, but fellow-workers, and each will do his best for his brothers and his own city. And your King shall be your servant!'

I don't know how they managed this, but no one seemed to think that there would be any difficulty about it when the King mentioned it; and when people really make up their minds to do anything, difficulties do most oddly disappear.

Wonderful rejoicings there were. The city was hung with flags and lamps. Bands played – the performers a little out of practice, because, of course, crows can't play the flute or the violin or the trombone – but the effect was very gay indeed. Then came the time – it was quite dark – when the King rose up on his throne and spoke; and Elsie, among all her new friends, listened with them to his words.

'Our deliverer Elsie', he said, 'was brought hither by the good magic of our Chief Mage and Prime Minister. She has removed the enchantment that held us; and the dragon, now that he has had his tea and recovered from the shock of being kindly treated, turns out to be the second strongest magician in the world – and he will help us and advise us, so long as we remember that we are all brothers and fellow-workers. And now comes the time when our Elsie must return to her own place, or another go in her stead. But we cannot send back our heroine, our deliverer.' (*Long, loud cheering.*) 'So one shall take her place. My daughter –'

The end of the sentence was lost in shouts of admiration. But Elsie stood up, small and white in her black frock, and said, 'No thank you. Perdona would simply hate it. And she doesn't know my daddy. He'll fetch me away from Mrs Staines some day . . .'

The thought of her daddy, far away in India, of the loneliness of Willow Farm, where now it would be night in that horrible bare attic where the poor dead untameable little mouse was, nearly choked Elsie. It was so bright and light and good and kind here. And India was so far away. Her voice stayed a moment on a broken note.

'I – I . . .' Then she spoke firmly.

'Thank you all so much,' she said – 'so very much. I do love you all, and it's lovely here. But, please, I'd like to go home now.'

The Prime Minister, in a silence full of love and understanding, folded his dark cloak round her.

It was dark in the attic. Elsie, crouching alone in the blackness by the fireplace where the dead mouse had been, put out her hand to touch its cold fur.

*

There were wheels on the gravel outside – the knocker swung strongly – '*Rat*-tat-tat-tat – *Tat! Tat!*' A pause – voices – hasty feet in strong boots sounded on the stairs, the key turned in the lock. The door opened a dazzling crack, then fully, to the glare of a lamp carried by Mrs Staines.

'Come down at once. I'm sure you're good now,' she said, in a great hurry and in a new honeyed voice.

But there were other feet on the stairs – a step that Elsie knew. 'Where's my girl?' the voice she knew cried cheerfully. But under the cheerfulness Elsie heard something other and dearer. 'Where's my girl?'

After all, it take less than a month to come from India to the house in England where one's heart is.

Out of the bare attic and the darkness Elsie leapt into light, into arms she knew. 'Oh, my daddy, my daddy!' she cried. 'How glad I am I came back!'

9

The Related Muff

We had never seen our cousin Sidney till that Christmas Eve, and we didn't want to see him then, and we didn't like him when we did see him. He was just dumped down into the middle of us by mother, at a time when it would have been unkind to her to say how little we wanted him.

We knew already that there wasn't to be any proper Christmas for us, because Aunt Ellie – the one who always used to send the necklaces and carved things from India, and remembered everybody's birthday – had come home ill. Very ill she was, at a hotel in London, and mother had to go to her, and, of course, father was away with his ship.

And then after we had said goodbye to mother, and told her how sorry we were, we were left to ourselves, and told each other what a shame it was, and no presents or anything. And then mother came suddenly back in a cab, and we all shouted 'Hooray' when we saw the cab stop, and her get out of it. And then we saw she was getting something out of the cab, and our hearts leapt up like the man's in the piece of school poetry when he beheld a rainbow in the sky – because we thought she had remembered about the presents, and the thing she was getting out of the cab was *them*.

Of course it was not – it was Sidney, very thin and yellow, and looking as sullen as a pig.

We opened the front door. Mother didn't even come in. She just said, 'Here's your Cousin Sidney. Be nice to him and give him a good time, there's darlings. And don't forget he's your visitor, so be very extra nice to him.'

I have sometimes thought it was the fault of what mother said about the visitor that made what did happen happen, but I am almost sure really that it was the fault of us, though I did not see it at the time, and even now I'm sure we didn't mean to be unkind. Quite the opposite. But the events of life are very confusing, especially when you try to think what made you do them, and whether you really meant to be naughty or not. Quite often it is not – but it turns out just the same.

When the cab had carried mother away – Hilda said it was like a dragon carrying away a queen – we said, 'How do you do,' to our Cousin Sidney, who replied, 'Quite well, thank you.'

And then, curiously enough, no one could think of anything more to say.

Then Rupert – which is me – remembered that about being a visitor, and he said:

'Won't you come into the drawing-room?'

He did when he had taken off his gloves and overcoat. There was a fire in the drawing-room, because we had been going to have games there with mother, only the telegram came about Aunt Ellie.

So we all sat on chairs in the drawing-room, and thought of nothing to say harder than ever.

Hilda did say, 'How old are you?' but, of course, we knew the answer to that. It was ten.

And Hugh said, 'Do you like England or India best?'

And our cousin replied, 'India ever so much, thank you.'

I never felt such a duffer. It was awful. With all the millions of interesting things that there are to say at other times, and I couldn't think of one. At last I said, 'Do you like games?'

And our cousin replied, 'Some games I do,' in a tone that made me sure that the games he liked wouldn't be our kind, but some wild Indian sort that we didn't know.

I could see that the others were feeling just like me, and I knew we could not go on like this till tea-time. And yet I didn't see any other way to go on in. It was Hilda who cut the Gorgeous knot at last. She said:

'Hugh, let you and I go and make a lovely surprise for Rupert and Sidney.'

And before I could think of any way of stopping them without being downright rude to our new cousin, they had fled the scene, just like any old conspirators. Rupert – me, I mean – was left alone with the stranger. I said:

'Is there anything you'd like to do?'

And he said, 'No, thank you.'

Then neither of us said anything for a bit – and I could hear the others shrieking with laughter in the hall.

I said, 'I wonder what the surprise will be like.'

He said, 'Yes, I wonder;' but I could tell from his tone that he did not wonder a bit.

The others were yelling with laughter. Have you ever noticed how very amused people always are when you're not there? If you're in bed – ill, or in disgrace, or anything – it always sounds like far finer jokes than ever occur when you are not out of things.

'Do you like reading?' said I – who am Rupert – in the tones of despair.

'Yes,' said the cousin.

'Then take a book,' I said hastily, for I really could not stand it another second, 'and you just read till the surprise is ready. I think I ought to go and help the others. I'm the eldest, you know.'

I did not wait – I suppose if you're ten you can choose a book for yourself – and I went.

Hilda's idea was just Indians, but I thought a wigwam would be nice. So we made one with the hall table and the fur rugs off the floor. If everything had been different, and Aunt Ellie hadn't been ill, we were to have had turkey for dinner.

The turkey's feathers were splendid for Indians, and the striped blankets off Hugh's and my beds, and all mother's beads. The hall is big like a room, and there was a fire. The afternoon passed like a beautiful dream. When Rupert had done his own feathering and blanketing, as well as brown paper moccasins, he helped the others. The tea-bell rang before we were quite dressed. We got Louisa to go up and tell our cousin that the surprise was ready, and we all got inside the wigwam. It was a very tight fit, with the feathers and the blankets.

He came down the stairs very slowly, reading all the time, and when he got to the mat at the bottom of the stairs we burst forth in all our war-paint from the wigwam. It upset, because Hugh and Hilda stuck between the table's legs, and it fell on the stone floor with quite a loud noise. The wild Indians picked themselves up out of the ruins and did the finest war-dance I've ever seen in front of my cousin Sidney.

He gave one little scream, and then sat down suddenly on the bottom steps. He leaned his head against the banisters and we thought he was admiring the war-dance, till Eliza, who had been laughing and making as much noise as anyone, suddenly went up to him and shook him.

'Stop that noise,' she said to us, 'he's gone off into a dead faint.'

He had.

Of course we were very sorry and all that, but

we never thought he'd be such a muff as to be frightened of three Red Indians and a wigwam that happened to upset. He was put to bed, and we had our teas.

'I wish we hadn't,' Hilda said.

'So do I,' said Hugh.

But Rupert said, 'No one *could* have expected a cousin of ours to be a chicken-hearted duffer. He's a muff. It's bad enough to have a muff in the house at all, and at Christmas time, too. But a related muff!'

Still the affair had cast a gloom, and we were glad when it was bed-time.

Next day was Christmas Day, and no presents, and nobody but the servants to wish a Merry Christmas to.

Our cousin Sidney came down to breakfast, and as it was Christmas Day Rupert bent his proud spirit to own he was sorry about the Indians.

Sidney said, 'It doesn't matter. I'm sorry too. Only I didn't expect it.'

We suggested two or three games, such as Parlour Cricket, National Gallery, and Grab – but Sidney said he would rather read. So we said would he mind if we played out the Indian game which we had dropped, out of politeness, when he fainted.

He said:

'I don't mind at all, now I know what it is you're up to. No, thank you, I'd rather read,' he added, in reply to Rupert's unselfish offer to dress him for the part of Sitting Bull.

So he read *Treasure Island*, and we fought on the stairs with no casualties except the gas globes, and then we scalped all the dolls – putting on paper scalps first because Hilda wished it – and we scalped Eliza as she passed through the hall – hers was a white scalp with lacey stuff on it and long streamers.

And when it was beginning to get dark we thought of flying machines. Of course Sidney wouldn't play at that either, and Hilda and Hugh were contented with paper wings – there were some rolls of rather decent yellow and pink crinkled paper that mother had bought to make lampshades of. They made wings of this, and then they played at fairies up and down the stairs, while Sidney sat at the bottom of the stairs and went on reading *Treasure Island*. But Rupert was determined to have a flying machine, with real flipper-flappery wings, like at Hendon. So he got two brass fire-guards out of the spare room and mother's bedroom, and covered them with newspapers fastened on with string. Then he got a tea-tray and fastened it on to himself with rug-straps, and then he slipped his arms in between the string and the fire-guards, and went to the top of the stairs and shouting, 'Look out below there! Beware Flying Machines!' He sat down suddenly on the tray, and tobogganed gloriously down the stairs, flapping his fire-guard wings. It was a great success, and felt more like flying than anything he ever played at. But Hilda had not had time to look out thoroughly, because he did not wait any time between his warning and his descent. So that she was still fluttering in the character of Queen of the Butterfly Fairies, about half-way down the stairs when the flying machine, composed of the two guards, the tea-tray, and Rupert, started from the top of them, and she could only get out of the way by standing back close against the wall. Unluckily the place where she was, was also the place where the gas was burning in a little recess. You remember we had broken the globe when we were playing Indians.

Now, of course, you know what happened, because you have read *Harriett and the Matches*, and all the rest of the stories that have been written to persuade children not to play with fire. No one was playing with fire that day, it is true, or doing anything really naughty at all – but however naughty we had been the thing that happened couldn't have been much worse. For the flying machine as it came rushing round the curve of the staircase banged against the legs of Hilda. She screamed and stumbled back. Her pink paper wings went into the gas that hadn't a globe. They flamed up, her hair frizzled, and her lace collar caught fire. Rupert could not do anything because he was held fast in his flying machine, and he and it were rolling painfully on the mat at the bottom of the stairs.

Hilda screamed.

I have since heard that a great yellow light fell on the pages of *Treasure Island*.

Next moment *Treasure Island* went spinning across the room. Sidney caught up the fur rug that was part of the wigwam, and as Hilda, screaming horribly, and with wings not of paper but of flames, rushed down the staircase, and stumbled over the flying machine, Sidney threw the rug over her, and rolled her over and over on the floor.

'Lie down!' he cried. 'Lie down! It's the only way.'

But somehow people never will lie down when their clothes are on fire, any more than they will lie still in the water if they think they are drowning, and someone is trying to save them. It came to something very like a fight. Hilda fought and struggled. Rupert got out of his fire-guards and added himself and his tea-tray to the scrimmage. Hugh slid down to the knob of the banisters and sat there yelling. The servants came rushing in.

But by that time the fire was out. And Sidney gasped out, 'It's all right. You aren't burned, Hilda, are you?'

Hilda was much too frightened to know whether she was burnt or not, but Eliza looked her over, and it turned out that only her neck was a little scorched, and a good deal of her hair frizzled off short.

Everyone stood, rather breathless and pale, and

everyone's face was much dirtier than customary, except Hugh's, which he had, as usual, dirtied thoroughly quite early in the afternoon. Rupert felt perfectly awful, ashamed and proud and rather sick. 'You're a regular hero, Sidney,' he said – and it was not easy to say – 'and yesterday I said you were a related muff. And I'm jolly sorry I did. Shake hands, won't you?'

Sidney hesitated.

'Too proud?' Rupert's feelings were hurt, and I should not wonder if he spoke rather fiercely.

'It's – it's a little burnt, I think,' said Sidney, 'don't be angry,' and he held out the left hand.

Rupert grasped it.

'I do beg your pardon,' he said, 'you *are* a hero!'

Sidney's hand was bad for ever so long, but we were tremendous chums after that.

It was when they'd done the hand up with scraped potato and salad oil – a great, big, fat, wet plaster of it – that I said to him:

'I don't care if you don't like games. Let's be pals.'

And he said, 'I do like games, but I couldn't care about anything with mother so ill. I know you'll think I'm a muff, but I'm not really, only I do love her so.'

And with that he began to cry, and I thumped him on the back, and told him exactly what a beast I knew I was, to comfort him.

When Aunt Ellie was well again we kept Christmas on the 6th of January, which used to be Christmas Day in middle-aged times.

Father came home before New Year, and he had a silver medal made, with a flame on one side, and on the other Sidney's name, and 'For Bravery'.

If I had not been tied up in fire-guards and tea-trays perhaps I should have thought of the rug and got the medal. But I do not grudge it to Sidney. He deserved it. And he is not a muff. I see now that a person might very well be frightened at finding Indians in the hall of a strange house, especially if the person had just come from the kind of India where the Indians are quite a different sort, and much milder, with no feathers and wigwams and war-dances, but only dusky features and University Degrees.

10

THE AUNT AND AMABEL

It is not pleasant to be a fish out of water. To be a cat in water is not what anyone would desire. To be in a temper is uncomfortable. And no one can fully taste the joys of life if he is in a Little Lord Fauntleroy suit. But by far the most uncomfortable thing to be in is disgrace, sometimes amusingly called Coventry by the people who are not in it.

We have all been there. It is a place where the heart sinks and aches, where familiar faces are clouded and changed, where any remark that one may tremblingly make is received with stony silence or with the assurance that nobody wants to talk to such a naughty child. If you are only in disgrace, and not in solitary confinement, you will creep about a house that is like the one you have had such jolly times in, and yet as unlike it as a bad dream is to a June morning. You will long to speak to people, and be afraid to speak. You will wonder whether there is anything you can do that will change things at all. You have said you are sorry, and that has changed nothing. You will wonder whether you are to stay for ever in this desolate place, outside all hope and love and fun and happiness. And though it has happened before, and has always, in the end, come to an end, you can never be quite sure that this time it is not going to last for ever.

'It *is* going to last for ever,' said Amabel, who was eight. 'What shall I do? Oh, whatever shall I do?'

What she *had* done ought to have formed the subject of her meditations. And she had done what had seemed to her all the time, and in fact still seemed, a self-sacrificing and noble act. She was staying with an aunt – measles or a new baby, or the painters in the house, I forget which, the cause of her banishment. And the aunt, who was really a great-aunt and quite old enough to know better, had been grumbling about her head gardener to a lady who called in blue spectacles and a beady bonnet with violet flowers in it.

'He hardly lets me have a plant for the table,' said the aunt, 'and that border in front of the breakfast-room window – it's just bare earth – and I expressly ordered chrysanthemums to be planted there. He thinks of nothing but his greenhouse.'

The beady-violet-blue-glassed lady snorted, and said she didn't know what we were coming to, and she would have just half a cup, please, with not quite so much milk, thank you very much.

Now what would you have done? Minded your own business most likely, and not got into trouble at all. Not so Amabel. Enthusiastically anxious to do something which should make the great-aunt see what a thoughtful, unselfish, little girl she really was (the aunt's opinion of her being at present quite otherwise), she got up very early in the morning and took the cutting-out scissors from the work-room table drawer and stole, 'like an errand of mercy', she told herself, to the green-house where she busily snipped off every single flower she could find. MacFarlane was at his breakfast. Then with the points of the cutting-out scissors she made nice deep little holes in the flower-bed where the chrysanthemums ought to have been, and struck the flowers in – chrysan-themums, geraniums, primulas, orchids and car-nations. It would be a lovely surprise for Auntie.

Then the aunt came down to breakfast and saw the lovely surprise. Amabel's world turned upside down and inside out suddenly and surprisingly, and there she was, in Coventry, and not even the housemaid would speak to her. Her great-uncle, whom she passed in the hall on her way to her own room, did indeed, as he smoothed his hat, murmur, 'Sent to Coventry, eh? Never mind, it'll soon be over,' and went off to the City banging the front door behind him.

He meant well, but he did not understand.

Amabel understood, or she thought she did, and knew in her miserable heart that she was sent to Coventry for the last time, and that this time she would stay there.

'I don't care,' she said quite untruly. 'I'll never

try to be kind to anyone again.' And that wasn't true either. She was to spend the whole day alone in the best bedroom, the one with the four-post bed and the red curtains and the large wardrobe with a looking-glass in it that you could see your-self in to the very ends of your strap-shoes.

The first thing Amabel did was to look at herself in the glass. She was still sniffing and sobbing, and her eyes were swimming in tears, another one rolled down her nose as she looked – that was very interesting. Another rolled down, and that was the last, because as soon as you get interested in watching your tears they stop.

Next she looked out of the window, and saw the decorated flower-bed, just as she had left it, very bright and beautiful.

'Well, it *does* look nice,' she said. 'I don't care what they say.'

Then she looked round the room for something to read; there was nothing. The old-fashioned best bedrooms never did have anything. Only on the large dressing-table, on the left-hand side of the oval swing-glass, was one book covered in red velvet, and on it, very twistily embroidered in yellow silk and mixed up with misleading leaves and squiggles were the letters, ABC.

'Perhaps it's a picture alphabet,' said Mabel, and was quite pleased, though of course she was much too old to care for alphabets. Only when one is very unhappy and very dull, anything is better than nothing. She opened the book.

'Why, it's only a time-table!' she said. 'I suppose it's for people when they want to go away, and Auntie puts it here in case they suddenly make up their minds to go, and feel that they can't wait another minute. I feel like that, only it's no good, and I expect other people do too.'

She had learned how to use the dictionary, and this seemed to go the same way. She looked up the names of all the places she knew – Brighton where she had once spent a month, Rugby where her brother was at school, and Home, which was Amberley – and she saw the times when the trains left for these places, and wished she could go by those trains.

And once more she looked round the best bedroom which was her prison, and thought of the Bastille, and wished she had a load to tame, like the poor Viscount, or a flower to watch growing, like Picciola, and she was very sorry for herself, and very angry with her aunt, and very grieved at the conduct of her parents – she had expected better things from them – and now they had left her in this dreadful place where no one loved her, and no one understood her.

There seemed to be no place for toads or flowers in the best room, it was carpeted all over even in its least noticeable corners. It had everything a best room ought to have – and everything was of dark shining mahogany. The toilet-table had a set of red and gold glass things – a tray, candlesticks, a ring-stand, many little pots with lids, and two bottles with stoppers. When the stoppers were taken out they smelt very strange, something like very old scent, and something like cold cream also very old, and something like going to the dentist's.

I do not know whether the scent of those bottles had anything to do with what happened. It certainly was a very extraordinary scent. Quite different from any perfume that I smell nowadays, but I remember that when I was a little girl I smelt it quite often. But then there are no best rooms now such as there used to be. The best rooms now are gay with chintz and mirrors, and there are always flowers and books, and little tables to put your teacup on, and sofas, and armchairs. And they smell of varnish and new furniture.

When Amabel had sniffed at both bottles and looked in all the pots, which were quite clean and empty except for a pearl button and two pins in one of them, she took up the ABC again to look for Whitby, where her godmother lived. And it was then that she saw the extraordinary name '*Whereyouwantogoto*'. This was odd – but the name of the station from which it started was still more extraordinary, for it was not Euston or Cannon Street or Marylebone.

The name of the station was '*Bigwardrobeinspareroom*'. And below this name, really quite unusual for a station, Amabel read in small letters:

'Single fares strictly forbidden. Return tickets

No Class Nuppence. Trains leave *Bigwardrobein-spareroom* all the time.'

And under that in still smaller letters:

'*You had better go now.*'

What would you have done? Rubbed your eyes and thought you were dreaming? Well, if you had, nothing more would have happened. Nothing ever does when you behave like that. Amabel was wiser. She went straight to the Big Wardrobe and turned its glass handle.

'I expect it's only shelves and people's best hats,' she said. But she only said it. People often say what they don't mean, so that if things turn out as they don't expect, they can say 'I told you so,' but this is most dishonest to one's self, and being dishonest to one's self is almost worse than being dishonest to other people. Amabel would never have done it if she had been herself. But she was out of herself with anger and unhappiness.

Of course it wasn't hats. It was, most amazingly, a crystal cave, very oddly shaped like a railway station. It seemed to be lighted by stars, which is, of course, unusual in a booking office, and over the station clock was a full moon. The clock had no figures, only *Now* in shining letters all round it, twelve times, and the *Nows* touched, so the clock was bound to be always right. How different from the clock you go to school by!

A porter in white satin hurried forward to take Amabel's luggage. Her luggage was the ABC which she still held in her hand.

'Lots of time, Miss,' he said, grinning in a most friendly way, 'I *am* glad you're going. You *will* enjoy yourself! What a nice little girl you are!'

This was cheering. Amabel smiled.

At the pigeon-hole that tickets come out of, another person, also in white satin, was ready with a mother-of-pearl ticket, round, like a card counter.

'Here you are, Miss,' he said with the kindest smile, 'price nothing, and refreshments free all the way: It's a pleasure,' he added, 'to issue a ticket to a nice little lady like you.' The train was entirely of crystal, too, and the cushions were of white satin. There were little buttons such as you have for electric bells, and on them '*Whatyouwantoeat*', '*Whatyouwantodrink*', '*Whatyouwantoread*', in silver letters.

Amabel pressed all the buttons at once, and instantly felt obliged to blink. The blink over, she saw on the cushion by her side a silver tray with vanilla ice, boiled chicken and white sauce, almonds (blanched), peppermint creams, and mashed potatoes, and a long glass of lemonade – beside the tray was a book. It was Mrs Ewing's *Bad-tempered Family*, and it was bound in white vellum.

There is nothing more luxurious than eating while you read – unless it be reading while you eat. Amabel did both: they are not the same thing, as you will see if you think the matter over.

And just as the last thrill of the last spoonful of

ice died away, and the last full stop of the *Bad-tempered Family* met Amabel's eye, the train stopped, and hundreds of railway officials in white velvet shouted, '*Whereyouwantogoto!* Get out!'

A velvety porter, who was somehow like a silk-worm as well as like a wedding handkerchief sachet, opened the door.

'Now!' he said, 'come on out, Miss Amabel, unless you want to go to *Whereyoudon'twantogo to.*'

She hurried out, on to an ivory platform.

'Not on the ivory, if you please,' said the porter, 'the white Axminster carpet – it's laid down expressly for you.'

Amabel walked along it and saw ahead of her a crowd, all in white.

'What's all that?' she asked the friendly porter.

'It's the Mayor, dear Miss Amabel,' he said, 'with your address.'

'My address is The Old Cottage, Amberley,' she said, 'at least it used to be' – and found herself face to face with the Mayor. He was very like Uncle George, but he bowed low to her, which was not Uncle George's habit, and said:

'Welcome, dear little Amabel. Please accept this admiring address from the Mayor and burgesses and apprentices and all the rest of it, of Whereyouwantogoto.'

The address was in silver letters, on white silk, and it said:

'Welcome, dear Amabel. We know you meant

to please your aunt. It was very clever of you to think of putting the greenhouse flowers in the bare flower-bed. You couldn't be expected to know that you ought to ask leave before you touch other people's things.'

'Oh, but,' said Amabel quite confused, 'I did . . .'

But the band struck up, and drowned her words. The instruments of the band were all of silver, and the bandsmen's clothes of white leather. The tune they played was 'Cheero!'

Then Amabel found that she was taking part in a procession, hand in hand with the Mayor, and the band playing like mad all the time. The Mayor was dressed entirely in cloth of silver, and as they went along he kept saying, close to her ear:

'You have our sympathy, you have our sympathy,' till she felt quite giddy.

There was a flower show – all the flowers were white. There was a concert – all the tunes were old ones. There was a play called *Put yourself in her place*. And there was a banquet, with Amabel in the place of honour.

They drank her health in white wine whey, and then through the Crystal Hall of a thousand gleaming pillars, where thousands of guests, all in white, were met to do honour to Amabel, the shout went up – 'Speech, speech!'

I cannot explain to you what had been going on in Amabel's mind. Perhaps you know. Whatever it was it began like a very tiny butterfly in a box, that could not keep quiet, but fluttered, and fluttered, and fluttered. And when the Mayor rose and said:

'Dear Amabel, you whom we all love and understand; dear Amabel, you who were so unjustly punished for trying to give pleasure to an unresponsive aunt; poor, ill-used, ill-treated, innocent Amabel; blameless, suffering Amabel, we await your words,' that fluttering, tiresome butterfly-thing inside her seemed suddenly to swell to the size and strength of a fluttering albatross, and Amabel got up from her seat of honour on the throne of ivory and silver and pearl, and said, choking a little, and extremely red about the ears:

'Ladies and gentlemen, I don't want to make a speech, I just want to say, "Thank you", and to say – to say – to say . . .'

She stopped, and all the white crowd cheered.

'To say,' she went on as the cheers died down, 'that I wasn't blameless, and innocent, and all those nice things. I ought to have thought. And they *were* Auntie's flowers. But I did want to please her. It's all so mixed. Oh, I wish Auntie was here!'

And instantly Auntie *was* there, very tall and quite nice-looking, in a white velvet dress and an ermine cloak.

'Speech,' cried the crowd. 'Speech from Auntie!'

Auntie stood on the step of the throne beside Amabel, and said:

'I think, perhaps, I was hasty. And I think Amabel meant to please me. But all the flowers that were meant for the winter . . . well – I was annoyed. I'm sorry.'

'Oh, Auntie, so am I – so am I,' cried Amabel, and the two began to hug each other on the ivory step, while the crowd cheered like mad, and the band struck up that well-known air, 'If you only understood!'

'Oh, Auntie,' said Amabel among hugs, 'This is such a lovely place, come and see everything, we may, mayn't we?' she asked the Mayor.

'The place is yours,' he said, 'and now you can see many things that you couldn't see before. We are The People who Understand. And now you are one of Us. And your aunt is another.'

I must not tell you all that they saw because these things are secrets only known to The People who Understand, and perhaps you do not yet belong to that happy nation. And if you do, you will know without my telling you.

And when it grew late, and the stars were drawn down, somehow, to hang among the trees, Amabel fell asleep in her aunt's arms beside a white foaming fountain on a marble terrace, where white peacocks came to drink.

She awoke on the big bed in the spare room, but her aunt's arms were still round her.

'Amabel,' she was saying, 'Amabel!'

'Oh, Auntie,' said Amabel sleepily, 'I am so sorry. It *was* stupid of me. And I did mean to please you.'

'It *was* stupid of you,' said the aunt, 'but I am sure you meant to please me. Come down to supper.' And Amabel has a confused recollection of her aunt's saying that she was sorry, adding, 'Poor little Amabel.'

If the aunt really did say it, it was fine of her. And Amabel is quite sure that she did say it.

Amabel and her great-aunt are now the best of friends. But neither of them has ever spoken to the other of the beautiful city called *Whereyouwantogoto*. Amabel is too shy to be the first to mention it, and no doubt the aunt has her own reasons for not broaching the subject.

But of course they both know that they have been there together, and it is easy to get on with people when you and they alike belong to the *Peoplewhounderstand*.

If you look in the ABC that your people have you will not find *'Whereyouwantogoto'*. It is only in the red velvet bound copy that Amabel found in her aunt's best bedroom.

11

KENNETH AND THE CARP

Kenneth's cousins had often stayed with him, but he had never till now stayed with them. And you know how different everything is when you are in your own house. You are certain exactly what games the grown-ups dislike and what games they will not notice; also what sort of mischief is looked over and what sort is not. And, being accustomed to your own sort of grown-ups, you can always be pretty sure when you are likely to catch it. Whereas strange houses are, in this matter of catching it, full of the most unpleasing surprises.

You know all this. But Kenneth did not. And still less did he know what were the sort of things which, in his cousins' house, led to disapproval, punishment, scoldings; in short, to catching it. So that that business of cousin Ethel's jewel-case, which is where this story ought to begin, was really not Kenneth's fault at all. Though for a time . . . But I am getting on too fast.

Kenneth's cousins were four – Conrad, Alison, George, and Ethel. The first three were natural sort of cousins somewhere near his own age, but Ethel was hardly like a cousin at all, more like an aunt, because she was grown-up. She wore long dresses and all her hair on the top of her head, a mass of combs and hairpins; in fact she had just had her twenty-first birthday with iced cakes and a party and lots of presents, most of them jewellery. And that brings me again to that affair of the jewel-case, or would bring me if I were not determined to tell things in their proper order, which is the first duty of a storyteller.

Kenneth's home was in Kent, a wooden house among cherry orchards, and the nearest river five miles away. That was why he looked forward in such a very extra and excited way to his visit to his cousins. Their house was very old, red brick with ivy all over it. It had a secret staircase, only the secret was not kept any longer, and the housemaids carried pails and brooms up and down the staircase. And the house was surrounded by a real deep moat, with clear water in it, and long weeds and water-lilies and fish – the gold and the silver and the everyday kinds.

The first evening of Kenneth's visit passed uneventfully. His bedroom window looked over the moat, and early next morning he tried to catch fish with several pieces of string knotted together and a hairpin kindly lent to him by the parlourmaid. He did not catch any fish, partly because he baited the hairpin with brown windsor soap, and it washed off.

'Besides, fish hate soap,' Conrad told him, 'and that hook of yours would do for a whale perhaps.

Only we don't stock our moat with whales. But I'll ask father to lend you his rod, it's a spiffing one, much jollier than ours. And I won't tell the kids because they'd never let it down on you. Fishing with a hairpin!'

'Thank you very much,' said Kenneth, feeling that his cousin was a man and a brother. The kids were only two or three years younger than he was, but that is a great deal when you are the elder; and besides, one of the kids was a girl.

'Alison's a bit of a sneak,' Conrad used to say when anger overcame politeness and brotherly feeling. Afterwards, when the anger was gone and the other things left, he would say, 'You see she went to a beastly school for a bit, at Brighton, for her health. And father says they must have bullied her. All girls are not like it, I believe.'

But her sneakish qualities, if they really existed, were generally hidden, and she was very clever at thinking of new games, and very kind if you got into a row over anything.

George was eight and stout. He was not a sneak, but concealment was foreign to his nature, so he never could keep a secret unless he forgot it. Which fortunately happened quite often.

The uncle very amiably lent Kenneth his fishing-rod, and provided real bait in the most thoughtful and generous manner. And the four children fished all the morning and all the afternoon. Conrad caught two roach and an eel. George caught nothing, and nothing was what the other two caught. But it was glorious sport. And the next day there was to be a picnic. Life to Kenneth seemed full of new and delicious excitement.

In the evening the aunt and the uncle went out to dinner, and Ethel, in her grown-up way, went with them, very grand in a blue silk dress and turquoises. So the children were left to themselves.

You know the empty hush which settles down on a house when the grown-ups have gone out to dinner and you have the whole evening to do what you like in. The children stood in the hall a moment after the carriage wheels had died away with the scrunching swish that the carriage wheels always made as they turned the corner by the lodge, where the gravel was extra thick and soft owing to the droppings from the trees. From the kitchen came the voices of the servants, laughing and talking.

'It's two hours at least to bedtime,' said Alison. 'What shall we do?' Alison always began by saying 'What shall we do?' and always ended by deciding what should be done. 'You all say what you think,' she went on, 'and then we'll vote about it. You first, Ken, because you're the visitor.'

'Fishing,' said Kenneth, because it was the only thing he could think of.

'Make toffee,' said Conrad.

'Build a great big house with all the bricks,' said George.

'We can't make toffee,' Alison explained gently

but firmly, 'because you know what the pan was like last time, and cook said, "never again, not much". And it's no good building houses, Georgie, when you could be out of doors. And fishing's simply rotten when we've been at it all day. I've thought of something.'

So of course all the others said, 'What?'

'We'll have a pageant, a river pageant, on the moat. We'll all dress up and hang Chinese lanterns in the trees. I'll be the Sunflower lady that the Troubadour came all across the sea, because he loved her so, for, and one of you can be the Troubadour, and the others can be sailors or anything you like.'

'I shall be the Troubadour,' said Conrad with decision.

'I think you ought to let Kenneth because he's the visitor,' said George, who would have liked to be it immensely himself, or anyhow did not see why Conrad should be a troubadour if *he* couldn't.

Conrad said what manners required, which was:

'Oh! all right, I don't care about being the beastly Troubadour.'

'You might be the Princess's brother,' Alison suggested.

'Not me,' said Conrad scornfully, 'I'll be the captain of the ship.'

'In a turban the brother would be, with the Benares cloak, and the Persian dagger out of the cabinet in the drawing-room,' Alison went on unmoved.

'I'll be that,' said George.

'No, you won't, I shall, so there,' said Conrad. 'You can be the captain of the ship.'

(But in the end both boys were captains, because that meant being on the boat, whereas being the Princess's brother, however turbanned, only meant standing on the bank. And there is no rule to prevent captains wearing turbans and Persian daggers, except in the Navy where, of course, it is not done.)

So then they all tore up to the attic where the dressing-up trunk was, and pulled out all the dressing-up things on to the floor. And all the time they were dressing, Alison was telling the others what they were to say and do. The Princess wore a white satin skirt and a red flannel blouse and a veil formed of several motor scarves of various colours. Also a wreath of pink roses off one of Ethel's old hats, and a pair of pink satin slippers with sparkly buckles.

Kenneth wore a blue silk dressing-jacket and a yellow sash, a lace collar, and a towel turban. And the others divided between them an eastern dressing-gown, once the property of their grand-father, a black spangled scarf, very holey, a pair of red and white football stockings, a Chinese coat, and two old muslin curtains, which, rolled up, made turbans of enormous size and fierceness.

On the landing outside cousin Ethel's open door Alison paused and said, 'I say!'

'Oh! come on,' said Conrad, 'we haven't fixed the Chinese lanterns yet, and it's getting dark.'

'You go on,' said Alison, 'I've just thought of something.'

The children were allowed to play in the boat so long as they didn't loose it from its moorings. The painter was extremely long, and quite the effect of coming home from a long voyage was produced when the three boys pushed the boat out as far as it would go among the boughs of the beech-tree which overhung the water, and then reappeared in the circle of red and yellow light thrown by the Chinese lanterns.

'What ho! ashore there!' shouted the captain.

'What ho!' said a voice from the shore which, Alison explained, was disguised.

'We be three poor mariners,' said Conrad by a happy effort of memory, 'just newly come to shore. We seek news of the Princess of Tripoli.'

'She's in her palace,' said the disguised voice, 'wait a minute, and I'll tell her you're here. But what do you want her for? ("A poor minstrel of France") go on, Con.'

'A poor minstrel of France,' said Conrad, '(all right! I remember,) who has heard of the Princess's beauty has come to lay, to lay . . .'

'His heart,' said Alison.

'All right, I know. His heart at her something or other feet.'

'Pretty feet,' said Alison. 'I go to tell the Princess.'

Next moment from the shadows of the bank a radiant vision stepped into the circle of light, crying:

'Oh! Rudel, is it indeed thou? Thou art come at last. O welcome to the arms of the Princess!'

'What do I do now?' whispered Rudel (who was Kenneth) in the boat, and at the same moment Conrad and George said, as with one voice:

'My hat! Alison, won't you catch it!'

For at the end of the Princess's speech she had thrown back her veils and revealed a blaze of splendour. She wore several necklaces, one of seed pearls, one of topazes, and one of Australian shells, besides a string of amber and one of coral. And the front of the red flannel blouse was studded with brooches, in one at least of which diamonds gleamed. Each arm had one or two bracelets and on her clenched hands glittered as many rings as any Princess could wish to wear.

So her brothers had some excuse for saying, 'You'll catch it.'

'No, I shan't. It's my look out, anyhow. Do shut up,' said the Princess, stamping her foot. 'Now then, Ken, go ahead. Ken, you say, "Oh Lady, I faint with rapture!"'

'I faint with rapture,' said Kenneth stolidly. 'Now I land, don't I?'

He landed and stared at the jewelled hand the Princess held out.

'At last, at last,' she said, 'but you ought to say that, Ken. I say, I think I'd better be an eloping Princess, and then I can come in the boat. Rudel dies really, but that's so dull. Lead me to your ship, oh noble stranger! for you have won the Princess, and with you I will live and die. Give me your hand, can't you, silly, and do mind my train.'

So Kenneth led her to the boat, and with some difficulty, for the satin train got between her feet, she managed to flounder into the punt.

'Now you stand and bow,' she said. 'Fair Rudel, with this ring I thee wed,' she pressed a large amethyst ring into his hand, 'remember that the Princess of Tripoli is yours for ever. Now let's sing *Integer Vitae* because it's Latin.'

So they sat in the boat and sang. And presently the servants came out to listen and admire, and at the sound of the servants' approach the Princess veiled her shining splendour.

'It's prettier than wot the Coventry pageant was, so it is,' said the cook, 'but it's long past your bed times. So come on out of that there dangerous boat, there's dears.'

So then the children went to bed. And when the house was quiet again, Alison slipped down and put back Ethel's jewellery, fitting the things into their cases and boxes as correctly as she could. 'Ethel won't notice,' she thought, but of course Ethel did.

So that next day each child was asked separately

by Ethel's mother who had been playing with Ethel's jewellery. And Conrad and George said they would rather not say. This was a form they always used in that family when that sort of question was asked, and it meant, 'It wasn't me, and I don't want to sneak.'

And when it came to Alison's turn, she found to her surprise and horror that instead of saying, 'I played with them,' she had said, 'I would rather not say.'

Of course the mother thought that it was Kenneth who had had the jewels to play with. So when it came to his turn he was not asked the same question as the others, but his aunt said:

'Kenneth, you are a very naughty little boy to take your cousin Ethel's jewellery to play with.'

'I didn't,' said Kenneth.

'Hush! hush!' said the aunt, 'do not make your fault worse by untruthfulness. And what have you done with the amethyst ring?'

Kenneth was just going to say that he had given it back to Alison, when he saw that this would be sneakish. So he said, getting hot to the ears, 'You don't suppose I've stolen your beastly ring, do you, Auntie?'

'Don't you dare to speak to me like that,' the aunt very naturally replied. 'No, Kenneth, I do not think you would steal, but the ring is missing and it must be found.'

Kenneth was furious and frightened. He stood looking down and kicking the leg of the chair.

'You had better look for it. You will have plenty of time, because I shall not allow you to go to the picnic with the others. The mere taking of the jewellery was wrong, but if you had owned your fault and asked Ethel's pardon, I should have overlooked it. But you have told me an untruth and you have lost the ring. You are a very wicked child, and it will make your dear mother very unhappy when she hears of it. That her boy should be a liar. It is worse than being a thief!'

At this Kenneth's fortitude gave way, and he lost his head. 'Oh, don't,' he said, 'I didn't. I didn't. I didn't. Oh! don't tell mother I'm a thief and a liar. Oh! Aunt Effie, please, *please* don't.' And with that he began to cry.

Any doubts Aunt Effie might have had were settled by this outbreak. It was now quite plain to her that Kenneth had really intended to keep the ring.

'You will remain in your room till the picnic party has started,' the aunt went on, 'and then you must find the ring. Remember I expect it to be found when I return. And I hope you will be in a better frame of mind and really sorry for having been so wicked.'

'Mayn't I see Alison?' was all he found to say.

And the answer was, 'Certainly not. I cannot allow you to associate with your cousins. You are not fit to be with honest, truthful children.'

So they all went to the picnic, and Kenneth was left alone. When they had gone he crept down and wandered furtively through the empty rooms, ashamed to face the servants, and feeling almost as wicked as though he had really done something wrong. He thought about it all, over and over again, and the more he thought the more certain he was that he *had* handed back the ring to Alison last night when the voices of the servants were first heard from the dark lawn.

But what was the use of saying so? No one would believe him, and it would be sneaking anyhow. Besides, perhaps he *hadn't* handed it back to her. Or rather, perhaps he had handed it and she hadn't taken it. Perhaps it had slipped into the boat. He would go and see.

But he did not find it in the boat, though he turned up the carpet and even took up the boards to look. And then an extremely miserable little boy began to search for an amethyst ring in all sorts of impossible places, indoors and out. You know the hopeless way in which you look for things that you know perfectly well you will never find, the borrowed penknife that you dropped in the woods, for instance, or the week's pocket-money which slipped through that hole in your pocket as you went to the village to spend it.

The servants gave him his meals and told him to cheer up. But cheering up and Kenneth were, for the time, strangers. People in books never can eat when they are in trouble, but I have noticed myself that if the trouble has gone on for some hours, eating is really rather a comfort. You don't enjoy eating so much as usual, perhaps, but at any rate it is something to do, and takes the edge off your sorrow for a short time. And cook was sorry for Kenneth and sent him up a very nice dinner and a very nice tea. Roast chicken and gooseberry pie the dinner was, and for tea there was cake with almond icing on it.

The sun was very low when he went back wearily to have one more look in the boat for that detestable amethyst ring. Of course it was not there. And the picnic party would be home soon. And he really did not know what his aunt would do to him.

'Shut me up in a dark cupboard, perhaps,' he thought gloomily, 'or put me to bed all day tomorrow. Or give me lines to write out, thousands, and thousands, and thousands, and thousands, and thousands, of them.'

The boat, set in motion by his stepping into it, swung out to the full length of its rope. The sun was shining almost level across the water. It was a very still evening, and the reflections of the trees and of the house were as distinct as the house and the trees themselves. And the water was unusually clear. He could see the fish swimming about, and the sand and pebbles at the bottom of the moat. How clear and quiet it looked down there, and what fun the fishes seemed to be having.

'I wish I was a fish,' said Kenneth. 'Nobody punishes *them* for taking rings they *didn't* take.'

And then suddenly he saw the ring itself, lying

calm, and quiet, and round, and shining, on the smooth sand at the bottom of the moat.

He reached for the boat-hook and leaned over the edge of the boat trying to get up the ring on the boat-hook's point. Then there was a splash.

'Good gracious! I wonder what that is?' said cook in the kitchen, and dropped the saucepan with the welsh rabbit in it which she had just made for kitchen supper.

Kenneth had leaned out too far over the edge of the boat, the boat had suddenly decided to go the other way, and Kenneth had fallen into the water.

The first thing he felt was delicious coolness, the second that his clothes had gone, and the next thing he noticed was that he was swimming quite easily and comfortably under water, and that he had no trouble with his breathing, such as people who tell you not to fall into water seem to expect you to have. Also he could see quite well, which he had never been able to do under water before.

'I can't think,' he said to himself, 'why people make so much fuss about your falling into the water. I shan't be in a hurry to get out. I'll swim right round the moat while I'm about it.'

It was a very much longer swim than he expected, and as he swam he noticed one or two things that struck him as rather odd. One was that he couldn't see his hands. And another was that he couldn't feel his feet. And he met some enormous fishes, like great cod or halibut, they seemed.

He had had no idea that there were fresh-water fish of that size.

They towered above him more like men-o'-war than fish, and he was rather glad to get past them. There were numbers of smaller fishes, some about his own size, he thought. They seemed to be enjoying themselves extremely, and he admired the clever quickness with which they darted out of the way of the great hulking fish.

And then suddenly he ran into something hard and very solid, and a voice above him said crossly:

'Now then, who are you a-shoving of? Can't you keep your eyes open, and keep your nose out of gentlemen's shirt fronts?'

'I beg your pardon,' said Kenneth, trying to rub his nose, and not being able to. 'I didn't know people could talk under water,' he added very much astonished to find that talking under water was as easy to him as swimming there.

'Fish can talk under water, of course,' said the voice, 'if they didn't, they'd never talk at all: they certainly can't talk *out* of it.'

'But I'm not a fish,' said Kenneth, and felt himself grin at the absurd idea.

'Yes, you are,' said the voice, 'of course you're a fish,' and Kenneth, with a shiver of certainty, felt that the voice spoke the truth. He *was* a fish. He must have become a fish at the very moment when he fell into the water. That accounted for his not being able to see his hands or feel his feet.

Because of course his hands were fins and his feet were a tail.

'Who are you?' he asked the voice, and his own voice trembled.

'I'm the Doyen Carp,' said the voice. 'You must be a very new fish indeed or you'd know that. Come up, and let's have a look at you.'

Kenneth came up and found himself face to face with an enormous fish who had round staring eyes and a mouth that opened and shut continually. It opened square like a kit-bag, and it shut with an extremely sour and severe expression like that of an offended rhinoceros.

'Yes,' said the Carp, 'you *are* a new fish. Who put you in?'

'I fell in,' said Kenneth, 'out of the boat, but I'm not a fish at all, really I'm not. I'm a boy, but I don't suppose you'll believe me.'

'Why shouldn't I believe you?' asked the Carp wagging a slow fin. 'Nobody tells untruths under water.'

And if you come to think of it, no one ever does.

'Tell me your true story,' said the Carp very lazily. And Kenneth told it.

'Ah! these humans!' said the Carp when he had done. 'Always in such a hurry to think the worst of everybody!' He opened his mouth squarely and shut it contemptuously. 'You're jolly lucky, you are. Not one boy in a million turns into a fish, let me tell you.'

'Do you mean that I've got to *go on* being a fish?' Kenneth asked.

'Of course you'll go on being a fish as long as you stop in the water. You couldn't live here, you know, if you weren't.'

'I might if I was an eel,' said Kenneth, and thought himself very clever.

'Well, *be* an eel then,' said the Carp, and swam away sneering and stately. Kenneth had to swim his hardest to catch up.

'Then if I get out of the water, shall I be a boy again?' he asked panting.

'Of course, silly,' said the Carp, 'only you can't get out.'

'Oh! can't I?' said Kenneth the fish, whisked his tail and swam off. He went straight back to the amethyst ring, picked it up in his mouth, and swam into the shallows at the edge of the moat. Then he tried to climb up the slanting mud and on to the grassy bank, but the grass hurt his fins horribly, and when he put his nose out of the water, the air stifled him, and he was glad to slip back again. Then he tried to jump out of the water, but he could only jump straight up into the air, so of course he fell straight down again into the water. He began to be afraid, and the thought that perhaps he was doomed to remain for ever a fish was indeed a terrible one. He wanted to cry, but the tears would not come out of his eyes. Perhaps there was no room for any more water in the moat.

The smaller fishes called to him in a friendly
jolly way to come and play with them – they were
having a quite exciting game of follow-my-leader
among some enormous water-lily stalks that
looked like trunks of great trees. But Kenneth had
no heart for games just then.

He swam miserably round the moat looking for
the old Carp, his only acquaintance in this strange
wet world. And at last, pushing through a thick
tangle of water weeds, he found the great fish.

'Now then,' said the Carp testily, 'haven't you
any better manners than to come tearing a gentleman's bed-curtains like that?'

'I beg your pardon,' said Kenneth Fish, 'but I
know how clever you are. Do please help me.'

'What do you want now?' said the Carp, and
spoke a little less crossly.

'I want to get out. I want to go and be a boy
again.'

'But you must have said you wanted to be a
fish.'

'I didn't mean it, if I did.'

'You shouldn't say what you don't mean.'

'I'll try not to again,' said Kenneth humbly,
'but how can I get out?'

'There's only one way,' said the Carp rolling his
vast body over in his water bed, 'and a jolly
unpleasant way it is. Far better stay here and be a
good little fish. On the honour of a gentleman
that's the best thing you can do.'

'I want to get out,' said Kenneth again.

'Well then, the only way is . . . you know we always teach the young fish to look out for hooks so that they may avoid them. *You* must look out for a hook and *take it*. Let them catch you. On a hook.'

The Carp shuddered and went on solemnly, 'Have you strength? Have you patience? Have you high courage and determination? You will want them all. Have you all these?'

'I don't know what I've got,' said poor Kenneth, 'except that I've got a tail and fins, and I don't know a hook when I see it. Won't you come with me? Oh! dear Mr Doyen Carp, *do* come and show me a hook.'

'It will hurt you,' said the Carp, 'very much indeed. You take a gentleman's word for it.'

'I know,' said Kenneth, 'you needn't rub it in.'

The Carp rolled heavily out of his bed.

'Come on then,' he said, 'I don't admire your taste, but if you *want* a hook, well, the gardener's boy is fishing in the cool of the evening. Come on.'

He led the way with a steady stately movement.

'I want to take the ring with me,' said Kenneth, 'but I can't get hold of it. Do you think you could put it on my fin with your snout?'

'My what!' shouted the old Carp indignantly and stopped dead.

'Your nose, I meant,' said Kenneth. 'Oh! please don't be angry. It would be so kind of you if you would. Shove the ring on, I mean.'

'That will hurt too,' said the Carp, and Kenneth thought he seemed not altogether sorry that it should.

It did hurt very much indeed. The ring was hard and heavy, and somehow Kenneth's fin would not fold up small enough for the ring to slip over it, and the Carp's big mouth was rather clumsy at the work. But at last it was done. And then they set out in search of a hook for Kenneth to be caught with.

'I wish we could find one! I wish we could!' Kenneth Fish kept saying.

'You're just looking for trouble,' said the Carp. 'Well, here you are!'

Above them in the clear water hung a delicious-looking worm. Kenneth Boy did not like worms any better than you do, but to Kenneth Fish that worm looked most tempting and delightful.

'Just wait a sec,' he said, 'till I get that worm.'

'You little silly,' said the Carp, *that's the hook*. Take it.'

'Wait a sec,' said Kenneth again.

His courage was beginning to ooze out of his fin tips, and a shiver ran down him from gills to tail.

'If you once begin to think about a hook you never take it,' said the Carp.

'*Never?*' said Kenneth. 'Then . . . oh! goodbye!' he cried desperately, and snapped at the worm. A sharp pain ran through his head and he felt himself drawn up into the air, that stifling, choking, husky, thick stuff in which fish cannot breathe. And as he swung in the air the dreadful thought came to him, 'Suppose I don't turn into a boy again? Suppose I keep being a fish?' And then he wished he hadn't. But it was too late to wish that.

Everything grew quite dark, only inside his head there seemed to be a light. There was a wild, rushing, buzzing noise, then something in his head seemed to break and he knew no more.

When presently he knew things again, he was lying on something hard. Was he Kenneth Fish lying on a stone at the bottom of the moat, or Kenneth Boy lying somewhere out of the water? His breathing was all right, so he wasn't a fish out of water or a boy under it.

'He's coming to,' said a voice. The Carp's he thought it was. But next moment he knew it to be the voice of his aunt, and he moved his hand and felt grass in it. He opened his eyes and saw above him the soft grey of the evening sky with a star or two.

'Here's the ring, Aunt,' he said.

The cook had heard a splash and had run out just as the picnic party arrived at the front door. They had all rushed to the moat, and the uncle had pulled Kenneth out with the boat-hook. He had not been in the water more than three minutes, they said. But Kenneth knew better.

They carried him in, very wet he was, and laid him on the breakfast-room sofa, where the aunt with hurried thoughtfulness had spread out the uncle's mackintosh.

'Get some rough towels, Jane,' said the aunt. 'Make haste, do.'

'I got the ring,' said Kenneth.

'Never mind about the ring, dear,' said the aunt, taking his boots off.

'But you said I was a thief and a liar,' Kenneth said feebly, 'and it was in the moat all the time.'

'*Mother!*' It was Alison who shrieked. 'You didn't say that to him?'

'Of course I didn't,' said the aunt impatiently. She thought she hadn't, but then Kenneth thought she had.

'It was *me* took the ring,' said Alison, 'and I dropped it. I didn't say I hadn't. I only said I'd rather not say. Oh Mother! poor Kenneth!'

The aunt, without a word, carried Kenneth up to the bathroom and turned on the hot-water tap. The uncle and Ethel followed.

'Why didn't you own up, you sneak?' said Conrad to his sister with withering scorn.

'Sneak,' echoed the stout George.

'I meant to. I was only getting steam up,' sobbed Alison. 'I didn't know. Mother only told us she wasn't pleased with Ken, and so he wasn't to go to the picnic. Oh! what shall I do? What shall I do?'

'Sneak!' said her brothers in chorus, and left her to her tears of shame and remorse.

It was Kenneth who next day begged everyone

to forgive and forget. And as it was *his* day –
rather like a birthday, you know – when no one
could refuse him anything, all agreed that the
whole affair should be buried in oblivion. Everyone was tremendously kind, the aunt more so than
any one. But Alison's eyes were still red when in
the afternoon they all went fishing once more.
And before Kenneth's hook had been two minutes
in the water there was a bite, a very big fish, the
uncle had to be called from his study to land it.

'Here's a magnificent fellow,' said the uncle.
'Not an ounce less than two pounds, Ken. I'll
have it stuffed for you.'

And he held out the fish and Kenneth found
himself face to face with the Doyen Carp. There
was no mistaking that mouth that opened like a
kit-bag, and shut in a sneer like a rhinoceros's. Its
eye was most reproachful.

'Oh! no,' cried Kenneth, 'you helped me back
and I'll help you back,' and he caught the Carp
from the hands of the uncle and flung it out in the
moat.

'Your head's not quite right yet, my boy,' said
the uncle kindly. 'Hadn't you better go in and lie
down a bit?'

But Alison understood, for he had told her the
whole story. He had told her that morning before
breakfast while she was still in deep disgrace; to
cheer her up, he said. And, most disappointingly,
it made her cry more than ever.

'Your poor little fins,' she had said, 'and having

your feet tied up in your tail. And it was all my fault.'

'I liked it,' Kenneth had said with earnest politeness, 'it was a most awful lark.' And he quite meant what he said.

12

The Magician's Heart

We all have our weaknesses. Mine is mulberries. Yours, perhaps, motorcars. Professor Taykin's was christenings – royal christenings. He always expected to be asked to the christening parties of all the little royal babies, and of course he never was, because he was not a lord, or a duke, or a seller of bacon and tea, or anything really high-class, but merely a wicked magician, who by economy and strict attention to customers had worked up a very good business of his own. He had not always been wicked. He was born quite good, I believe, and his old nurse, who had long since married a farmer and retired into the calm of country life, always used to say that he was the duckiest little boy in a plaid frock with the dearest little fat legs. But he had changed since he was a boy, as a good many other people do – perhaps it was his trade. I dare say you've noticed that cobblers are usually thin, and brewers are generally fat, and magicians are almost always wicked.

Well, his weakness (for christenings) grew stronger and stronger because it was never indulged, and at last he 'took the bull into his own hands', as the Irish footman at the palace said, and went to a christening without being asked. It was a very grand party given by the King of the Fortunate Islands, and the little prince was christened Fortunatus. No one took any notice of Professor Taykin. They were too polite to turn him out, but they made him wish he'd never come. He felt quite an outsider, as indeed he was, and this made him furious. So that when all the bright, light, laughing, fairy god-mothers were crowding round the blue satin cradle, and giving gifts of beauty and strength and goodness to the baby, the Magician suddenly did a very difficult charm (in his head, like you do mental arithmetic), and said:

'Young Forty may be all that, but *I* say he shall be the stupidest prince in the world,' and on that he vanished in a puff of red smoke with a smell like the Fifth of November in a back garden on Streatham Hill, and as he left no address the King of the Fortunate Islands couldn't prosecute him for high treason.

Taykin was very glad to think that he had made such a lot of people unhappy – the whole Court was in tears when he left, including the baby – and he looked in the papers for another royal christening, so that he could go to that and make a lot more people miserable. And there was one fixed for the very next Wednesday. The Magician went to that, too, disguised as a wealthy.

This time the baby was a girl. Taykin kept close to the pink velvet cradle, and when all the nice qualities in the world had been given to the Princess he suddenly said, 'Little Aura may be all that, but *I* say she shall be the ugliest princess in all the world.'

And instantly she was. It was terrible. And she had been such a beautiful baby too. Everyone had been saying that she was the most beautiful baby they had ever seen. This sort of thing is often said at christenings.

Having uglified the unfortunate little Princess the Magician did the spell (in his mind, just as you do your spelling) to make himself vanish, but to his horror there was no red smoke and no smell of fireworks, and there he was, still, where he now very much wished not to be. Because one of the fairies there had seen, just one second too late to save the Princess, what he was up to, and had made a strong little charm in a great hurry to prevent his vanishing. This Fairy was a White Witch, and of course you know that White Magic is much stronger than Black Magic, as well as more suited for drawing-room performances. So there the Magician stood, 'looking like a thunder-struck pig', as someone unkindly said, and the dear White Witch bent down and kissed the baby princess.

'There!' she said, 'you can keep that kiss till you want it. When the time comes you'll know what to do with it. The Magician can't vanish, Sire. You'd better arrest him.'

'Arrest that person,' said the King, pointing to

Taykin. 'I suppose your charms are of a permanent nature, madam.'

'Quite,' said the Fairy, 'at least they never go till there's no longer any use for them.'

So the Magician was shut up in an enormously high tower, and allowed to play with magic; but none of his spells could act outside the tower so he was never able to pass the extra double guard that watched outside night and day. The King would have liked to have the Magician executed but the White Witch warned him that this would never do.

'Don't you see,' she said, 'he's the only person who can make the Princess beautiful again. And he'll do it some day. But don't you go *asking* him to do it. He'll never do anything to oblige you. He's that sort of man.'

So the years rolled on. The Magician stayed in the tower and did magic and was very bored – for it is dull to take white rabbits out of your hat, and your hat out of nothing when there's no one to see you.

Prince Fortunatus was such a stupid little boy that he got lost quite early in the story, and went about the country saying his name was James, which it wasn't. A baker's wife found him and adopted him, and sold the diamond buttons of his little overcoat, for three hundred pounds, and as she was a very honest woman she put two hundred away for James to have when he grew up.

The years rolled on. Aura continued to be

hideous, and she was very unhappy, till on her twentieth birthday her married cousin Belinda came to see her. Now Belinda had been made ugly in her cradle too, so she could sympathize as no one else could.

'But *I* got out of it all right, and so will you,' said Belinda. 'I'm sure the first thing to do is to find a magician.'

'Father banished them all twenty years ago,' said Aura behind her veil, 'all but the one who uglified me.'

'Then I should go to *him*,' said beautiful Belinda. 'Dress up as a beggar maid, and give him fifty pounds to do it. Not more, or he may suspect that you're not a beggar maid. It will be great fun. I'd go with you only I promised Bellamant faithfully that I'd be home to lunch.' And off she went in her mother-of-pearl coach, leaving Aura to look through the bound volumes of *The Perfect Lady* in the palace library, to find out the proper costume for a beggar maid.

Now that very morning the Magician's old nurse had packed up a ham, and some eggs, and some honey, and some apples, and a sweet bunch of old-fashioned flowers, and borrowed the baker's boy to hold the horse for her, and started off to see the Magician. It was forty years since she'd seen him, but she loved him still, and now she thought she could do him a good turn. She asked in the town for his address, and learned that he lived in the Black Tower.

'But you'd best be careful,' the townsfolk said, 'he's a spiteful chap.'

'Bless you,' said the old nurse, 'he won't hurt me as I nursed him when he was a babe, in a plaid frock with the dearest little fat legs ever you see.'

So she got to the tower, and the guards let her through. Taykin was almost pleased to see her – remember he had had no visitors for twenty years – and he was quite pleased to see the ham and the honey.

'But where did I put them *h*eggs?' said the nurse, 'and the apples – I must have left them at home after all.'

She had. But the Magician just waved his hand in the air, and there was a basket of apples that hadn't been there before. The eggs he took out of her bonnet, the folds of her shawl, and even from his own mouth, just like a conjurer does. Only of course he was a real Magician.

'Lor!' said she, 'it's like magic.'

'It *is* magic,' said he. 'That's my trade. It's quite a pleasure to have an audience again. I've lived here alone for twenty years. It's very lonely, especially of an evening.'

'Can't you get out?' said the nurse.

'No. King's orders must be respected, but it's a dog's life.' He sniffed, made himself a magic handkerchief out of empty air, and wiped his eyes.

'Take an apprentice, my dear,' said the nurse.

'And teach him my magic? Not me.'

'Suppose you got one so stupid he *couldn't* learn?'

'That would be all right – but it's no use advertising for a stupid person – you'd get no answers.'

'You needn't advertise,' said the nurse; and she went out and brought in James, who was really the Prince of the Fortunate Islands, and also the baker's boy she had brought with her to hold the horse's head.

'Now, James,' she said, 'you'd like to be apprenticed, wouldn't you?'

'Yes,' said the poor stupid boy.

'Then give the gentleman your money, James.'

James did.

'My last doubts vanish,' said the Magician, 'he *is* stupid. Nurse, let us celebrate the occasion with a little drop of something. Not before the boy because of setting an example. James, wash up. Not here, silly; in the back kitchen.'

So James washed up, and as he was very clumsy he happened to break a little bottle of essence of dreams that was on the shelf, and instantly there floated up from the washing-up water the vision of a princess more beautiful than the day – so beautiful that even James could not help seeing how beautiful she was, and holding out his arms to her as she came floating through the air above the kitchen sink. But when he held out his arms she vanished. He sighed and washed up harder than ever.

'I wish I wasn't so stupid,' he said, and then

there was a knock at the door. James wiped his hands and opened it. Someone stood there in very picturesque rags and tatters. 'Please,' said someone, who was of course the Princess, 'is Professor Taykin at home?'

'Walk in, please,' said James.

'My snakes alive!' said Taykin, 'what a day we're having. Three visitors in one morning. How kind of you to call. Won't you take a chair?'

'I hoped,' said the veiled Princess, 'that you'd give me something else to take.'

'A glass of wine,' said Taykin. 'You'll take a glass of wine?'

'No, thank you,' said the beggar maid who was the Princess.

'Then take . . . take your veil off,' said the nurse, 'or you won't feel the benefit of it when you go out.'

'I can't,' said Aura, 'it wouldn't be safe.'

'Too beautiful, eh?' said the Magician. 'Still – you're quite safe here.'

'Can you do magic?' she abruptly asked.

'A little,' said he ironically.

'Well,' said she, 'it's like this. I'm so ugly no one can bear to look at me. And I want to go as kitchenmaid to the palace. They want a cook and a scullion and a kitchenmaid. I thought perhaps you'd give me something to make me pretty. I'm only a poor beggar maid . . . It would be a great thing to me if . . .'

'Go along with you,' said Taykin, very cross indeed. 'I never give to beggars.'

'Here's twopence,' whispered poor James, pressing it into her hand, 'it's all I've got left.'

'Thank you,' she whispered back. 'You *are* good.'

And to the Magician she said:

'I happen to have fifty pounds. I'll give it you for a new face.'

'Done,' cried Taykin. 'Here's another stupid one!' He grabbed the money, waved his wand, and then and there before the astonished eyes of the nurse and the apprentice the ugly beggar maid became the loveliest princess in the world.

'Lor!' said the nurse.

'My dream!' cried the apprentice.

'Please,' said the Princess, 'can I have a looking-glass?' The apprentice ran to unhook the one that hung over the kitchen sink, and handed it to her. 'Oh,' she said, 'how *very* pretty I am. How can I thank you?'

'Quite easily,' said the Magician, 'beggar maid as you are, I hereby offer you my hand and heart.'

He put his hand into his waistcoat and pulled out his heart. It was fat and pink, and the Princess did not like the look of it.

'Thank you very much,' said she, 'but I'd rather not.'

'But I insist,' said Taykin.

'But really, your offer . . .'

'Most handsome, I'm sure,' said the nurse.

'My affections are engaged,' said the Princess, looking down. 'I can't marry you.'

'Am I to take this as a refusal?' asked Taykin; and the Princess said she feared that he was.

'Very well, then,' he said, 'I shall see you home, and ask your father about it. He'll not let you refuse an offer like this. Nurse, come and tie my necktie.'

So he went out, and the nurse with him.

Then the Princess told the apprentice in a very great hurry who she was.

'It would never do,' she said, 'for him to see me home. He'd find out that I was the Princess, and he'd uglify me again in no time.'

'He shan't see you home,' said James. 'I may be stupid but I'm strong too.'

'How brave you are,' said Aura admiringly, 'but I'd rather slip away quietly, without any fuss. Can't you undo the patent lock of that door?' The apprentice tried but he was too stupid, and the Princess was not strong enough.

'I'm sorry,' said the apprentice who was a Prince. 'I can't undo the door, but when *he* does I'll hold him and you can get away. I dreamed of you this morning,' he added.

'I dreamed of you too,' said she, 'but you were different.'

'Perhaps,' said poor James sadly, 'the person you dreamed about wasn't stupid, and I am.'

'Are you *really*?' cried the Princess. 'I *am* so glad!'

'That's rather unkind, isn't it?' said he.

'No; because if *that's* all that makes you different from the man I dreamed about I can soon make *that* all right.'

And with that she put her hands on his shoulders and kissed him. And at her kiss his stupidness passed away like a cloud, and he became as clever as anyone need be; and besides knowing all the ordinary lessons he would have learned if he had stayed at home in his palace, he knew who he was, and where he was, and why, and he knew all the geography of his father's kingdom, and the exports and imports and the condition of politics. And he knew also that the Princess loved him.

So he caught her in his arms and kissed her, and they were very happy, and told each other over and over again what a beautiful world it was, and how wonderful it was that they should have found each other, seeing that the world is not only beautiful but rather large.

'That first one was a magic kiss, you know,' said she. 'My fairy godmother gave it to me, and I've been keeping it all these years for you. You must get away from here, and come to the palace. Oh, you'll manage it – you're clever now.'

'Yes,' he said, 'I *am* clever now. I can undo the lock for you. Go, my dear, go before he comes back.'

So the Princess went. And only just in time; for as she went out of one door Taykin came in at the other.

He was furious to find her gone; and I should not like to write down the things he said to his apprentice when he found that James had been so stupid as to open the door for her. They were not polite things at all.

He tried to follow her. But the Princess had warned the guards, and he could not get out.

'Oh,' he cried, 'if only my old magic would work outside this tower. I'd soon be even with her.'

And then in a strange, confused, yet quite sure way, he felt that the spell that held him, the White Witch's spell, was dissolved.

'To the palace!' he cried; and rushing to the cauldron that hung over the fire he leaped into it, leaped out in the form of a red lion, and disappeared.

Without a moment's hesitation the Prince, who was his apprentice, followed him, calling out the same words and leaping into the same cauldron, while the poor nurse screamed and wrung her hands. As he touched the liquor in the cauldron he felt that he was not quite himself. He was, in fact, a green dragon. He felt himself vanish – a most uncomfortable sensation – and reappeared, with a suddenness that took his breath away, in his own form and at the back door of the palace.

The time had been short, but already the Magician had succeeded in obtaining an engagement as palace cook. How he did it without references I don't know. Perhaps he made the references by magic as he had made the eggs, and the apples, and the handkerchief.

Taykin's astonishment and annoyance at being followed by his faithful apprentice were soon soothed, for he saw that a stupid scullion would be of great use. Of course he had no idea that James had been made clever by a kiss.

'But how are you going to cook?' asked the apprentice. 'You don't know how!'

'I shall cook,' said Taykin, 'as I do everything else – by magic.' And he did. I wish I had time to tell you how he turned out a hot dinner of seventeen courses from totally empty saucepans, how James looked in a cupboard for spices and found it empty, and how next moment the nurse walked out of it. The Magician had been so long alone that he seemed to revel in the luxury of showing off to someone, and he leaped about from one cupboard to another, produced cats and cockatoos out of empty jars, and made mice and rabbits disappear and reappear till James's head was in a whirl, for all his cleverness; and the nurse, as she washed up, wept tears of pure joy at her boy's wonderful skill.

'All this excitement's bad for my heart, though,' Taykin said at last, and pulling his heart out of his chest, he put it on a shelf, and as he did so his magic note-book fell from his breast and the apprentice picked it up. Taykin did not see him do it; he was busy making the kitchen lamp fly about the room like a pigeon.

It was just then that the Princess came in, looking more lovely than ever in a simple little morning frock of white chiffon and diamonds.

'The beggar maid,' said Taykin, 'looking like a princess! I'll marry her just the same.'

'I've come to give the orders for dinner,' she said; and then she saw who it was, and gave one little cry and stood still, trembling.

'To order the dinner,' said the nurse. 'Then you're –'

'Yes,' said Aura, 'I'm the Princess.'

'You're the Princess,' said the Magician. 'Then I'll marry you all the more. And if you say no I'll uglify you as the word leaves your lips. Oh, yes – you think I've just been amusing myself over my cooking – but I've really been brewing the strongest spell in the world. Marry me – or drink –'

The Princess shuddered at these dreadful words.

'Drink, or marry me,' said the Magician. 'If you marry me you shall be beautiful for ever.'

'Ah,' said the nurse, 'he's a match even for a Princess.'

'I'll tell papa,' said the Princess, sobbing.

'No, you won't,' said Taykin. 'Your father will never know. If you won't marry me you shall drink this and become my scullery maid – my hideous scullery maid – and wash up for ever in the lonely tower.'

He caught her by the wrist.

'Stop,' cried the apprentice, who was a Prince.

'Stop? *Me?* Nonsense! Pooh!' said the Magician.

'Stop, I say!' said James, who was Fortunatus. '*I've got your heart!*' He had – and he held it up in one hand, and in the other a cooking knife.

'One step nearer that lady,' said he, 'and in goes the knife.'

The Magician positively skipped in his agony and terror.

'I say, look out!' he cried. 'Be careful what you're doing. Accidents happen so easily! Suppose your foot slipped! Then no apologies would meet the case. That's my heart you've got there. My life's bound up in it.'

'I know. That's often the case with people's hearts,' said Fortunatus. 'We've got you, my dear sir, on toast. My Princess, might I trouble you to call the guards.'

The Magician did not dare to resist, so the guards arrested him. The nurse, though in floods of tears, managed to serve up a very good plain dinner, and after dinner the Magician was brought before the King.

Now the King, as soon as he had seen that his daughter had been made so beautiful, had caused a large number of princes to be fetched by telephone. He was anxious to get her married at once in case she turned ugly again. So before he could do justice to the Magician he had to settle which of the princes was to marry the Princess. He had chosen the Prince of the Diamond Mountains, a very nice steady young man with a good income. But when he suggested the match to the Princess she declined it, and the Magician, who was standing at the foot of the throne steps loaded with chains, clattered forward and said:

'Your Majesty, will you spare my life if I tell you something you don't know?'

The King, who was a very inquisitive man, said 'Yes.'

'Then know,' said Taykin, 'that the Princess won't marry *your* choice, because she's made one of her own – my apprentice.'

The Princess meant to have told her father this when she had got him alone and in a good temper. But now he was in a bad temper, and in full audience.

The apprentice was dragged in, and all the Princess's agonized pleadings only got this out of the King:

'All right. I won't hang him. He shall be best man at your wedding.'

Then the King took his daughter's hand and set her in the middle of the hall, and set the Prince of the Diamond Mountains on her right and the apprentice on her left. Then he said:

'I will spare the life of this aspiring youth on your left if you'll promise never to speak to him again, and if you'll promise to marry the gentleman on your right before tea this afternoon.'

The wretched Princess looked at her lover, and his lips formed the word 'Promise.'

So she said: 'I promise never to speak to the gentleman on my left and to marry the gentleman on my right before tea today,' and held out her hand to the Prince of the Diamond Mountains.

Then suddenly, in the twinkling of an eye, the Prince of the Diamond Mountains was on her left, and her hand was held by her own Prince, who stood at her right hand. And yet nobody seemed to have moved. It was the purest and most high-class magic.

'Dished,' cried the King, 'absolutely dished!'

'A mere trifle,' said the apprentice modestly. 'I've got Taykin's magic recipe book, as well as his heart.'

'Well, we must make the best of it, I suppose,' said the King crossly. 'Bless you, my children.'

He was less cross when it was explained to him that the apprentice was really the Prince of the Fortunate Islands, and a much better match than the Prince of the Diamond Mountains, and he was in quite a good temper by the time the nurse threw herself in front of the throne and begged the King to let the Magician off altogether – chiefly on the ground that when he was a baby he was the dearest little duck that ever was, in the prettiest plaid frock, with the loveliest fat legs.

The King, moved by these arguments, said:

'I'll spare him if he'll promise to be good.'

'You will, ducky, won't you?' said the nurse, crying.

'No,' said the Magician, 'I won't; and what's more, I can't.'

The Princess, who was now so happy that she wanted everyone else to be happy too, begged her lover to make Taykin good 'by magic'.

'Alas, my dearest Lady,' said the Prince, 'no one can be made good by magic. I could take the badness out of him – there's an excellent recipe in this note-book – but if I did that there'd be so very little left.'

'Every little helps,' said the nurse wildly.

Prince Fortunatus, who was James, who was the apprentice, studied the book for a few moments, and then said a few words in a language no one present had ever heard before.

And as he spoke the wicked Magician began to tremble and shrink.

'Oh, my boy – be good! Promise you'll be good,' cried the nurse, still in tears.

The Magician seemed to be shrinking inside his clothes. He grew smaller and smaller. The nurse caught him in her arms, and still he grew less and less, till she seemed to be holding nothing but a bundle of clothes. Then with a cry of love and triumph she tore the Magician's clothes away and held up a chubby baby boy, with the very plaid frock and fat legs she had so often and so lovingly described.

'I said there wouldn't be much of him when the badness was out,' said the Prince Fortunatus.

'I will be good; oh, I will,' said the baby boy that had been the Magician.

'I'll see to that,' said the nurse. And so the story ends with love and a wedding, and showers of white roses.